# Sabine

DOROTHY TOPFER

**Sabine**

First published in Australia by Dorothy Topfer 2024
www.dorothy.topfer.com

 A catalogue record for this
book is available from the
National Library of Australia

ISBN: 978-0-6451559-4-5 (pbk)
ISBN: 978-0-6451559-5-2 (ebk)

Book cover photography by Stock Studio 4477 (shutterstock) ©

Typesetting and design by Publicious Book Publishing
Published in collaboration with Publicious Book Publishing
www.publicious.com.au

# Contents

Other titles by this author:

*Perfect Breaks*

*Past Presence*

Also available on Kindle:

*The Lost Spirit*

*Unravelling*

*The Legacy*

*Remembrance*

*The Life and Death of Gypsy Carmichael*

# Chapter One

# The Proposal

As usual she was late.

Sabine knew her arrival would be greeted by what she had come to call that look – the pointed glance at the designer wristwatch and the faint frown, before being greeted with a sighed comment referring to her failure to be anywhere on time.

It seemed to her like the entire day had been a disaster, with work deadlines not met and last-minute phone calls from irate clients. And now, as she raced to meet Max for a dinner date at some restaurant he preferred, she had the misfortune to be caught in one of those torrential downpours that were a speciality of a Sydney summer.

A concerned waiter greeted her as she sloshed into the restaurant – she suspected he would be worried about the impact on their floors by this sodden customer. A quick exchange of her drenched jacket for a warm towel and five minutes in the bathroom was enough she hoped to repair some of the damage from the storm. Her hair could be scraped back into a ponytail, her face towelled dry and judicious pointing of the hand dryer could remedy some of the rain damage to her clothing, but nothing could be done to disguise the squelching sound her shoes made as she approached Max, who was seated at the table staring gloomily down at his phone.

'Sorry I was late. It's been a horrible day at work and then I was caught in the most ferocious storm.'

She could feel herself tensing, in expectation of the usual criticism about tardiness and the need for punctuality but to her surprise, no such words were said. Instead, she was greeted with a smile and a kiss.

'Never mind that. You're here now. I've ordered for us – the shared seafood platter. And let me pour you some of this wine – it's not too bad for a house white.'

Sabine tried to smile as if in appreciation and forced herself not to react. Maybe it was a sign of his care for her that he would assume he knew what she would like to eat, but for once she would like to make her own selection from the menu. To say something now might appear to be ungracious, and after all she had been late. If only she had been on time.

Max took a deep breath as he looked intently into her face and spoke:

'Sabine,' and then he paused as if he had finally noticed her still damp appearance, 'you really did get soaked didn't you. Here, take this and wipe under your eyes – panda eyes only work for pandas you know.'

He smiled at his joke and passed across a perfectly pressed handkerchief. Of course, she thought, his handkerchiefs were like everything else he had - immaculate and of the best quality.

Once satisfied that her appearance was restored to rights, he resumed.

'Sabine. I wanted to see you tonight for a reason – a special reason. It's been a while. Although I knew what we have is special right from the very start, and I hope you feel the same way. But I think it's now time I…'

His words continued to swirl around Sabine – delivered in perfectly modulated tones, each word and sentence grammatically correct and spoken in what she thought was intended to be a sincere manner.

With increasing dread, Sabine realised that what she was hearing was a well thought out proposal – a proposal for marriage. Yet if this was a proposal from someone she truly loved, then why was it that all she could feel was the sensation of the ground falling away beneath her and the feeling of helpless falling into a bottomless pit?

# Chapter Two

# Many months earlier – the Judge's funeral

By all rights the day of a funeral should have been overcast and wet, with miserable weather in keeping with the mood of the mourners. But on this day somehow the weather gods had not received or had mislaid the message. For the day had dawned in glorious technicolour and continued that way. A perfect summer's day - not too hot and not too cold. The sky clear of clouds and a wayward breeze blowing in off the sea, its salty tang tantalizing with promises of the beach and a dive into welcoming waters.

Yet such siren calls were not to be heeded. There was the matter of a funeral to be witnessed. The service finally over and the chapel vacated, people now clustered in random groups outside in the forecourt quietly murmuring, now and then with the sounds of muffled laughter and exclamations as long-lost friends and casual acquaintances greeted each other.

Sabine stood quietly next to her mother and surveyed the crowd – a sea of black and a mass of people largely unknown to her. Her mother, she sensed was near to breaking point but to all appearances Anna was her usual elegant and composed self, exchanging polite words with those who lined up to greet her.

The words: *So sorry. He was a great man*, and *You must be so sad* floated around her like the motes of dust in the sunlit air. It was all so surreal. Surely this could not be happening and at any moment her father would appear – leaping out of the coffin left in centre stage inside the chapel, arms open wide, jubilant over the success of his latest trickery. A man larger than life could not die so quickly and so quietly in his study, at his desk one Sunday afternoon.

A sound, not from her father but closer. The sound of a throat clearing interrupted Sabine's thoughts. Her uncle, her father's brother, his imposing bulk and height dwarfing that of Sabine's mother by whose side he stood as he cleared his throat once again and then spoke to the crowd.

'On behalf of my sister-in-law I would like to thank you for your attendance on this very sad occasion. We would appreciate it if you would join us for some refreshments at the memorial hall across the road.' He pointed his arm towards the hall and heads turned in that direction as if in response.

Her uncle led the way as he escorted Sabine's mother towards the hall. For a moment Sabine could sense her mother's resistance and saw her stiffen as a reaction to his hand taking her arm. Then with the outtake of a breath like a sigh, all fight left her, and Anna allowed herself to be led away. A dainty figure clothed in a conservative black suit. Her upright posture and the gliding steps of a former dancer giving the outfit much more elegance than it deserved. Giving a grimace Sabine followed, feeling as she often did like an elephant following a gazelle. Her height and athletic build were inherited from her father and in fact nothing that she could discern had been inherited from her mother. Colouring – the same blonde hair and blue eyes as her father and his ancestors had displayed. Tall, long legged and altogether in keeping with the nickname from school – *Val* – short for Valkyrie. On the other hand, her mother, dark complexioned, doe-eyed, raven haired and with a dainty build seemed to invoke a protective response in everyone. Her father had always treated her with loving indulgence – *Don't fuss yourself Anna*, he would say. *Let someone else look after it. The staff can deal with it.* Constant reminders to Sabine not to upset her mother left Sabine with the impression that her mother was an exotic type of hothouse flower to be cosseted and protected – to be shielded from the challenges of every day worries and held out on display like some precious jewel or a rare find from a faraway country.

As a child this had seemed totally unexceptionable to Sabine. Wasn't everyone's mother treated like they needed special care? Sometimes she wondered what her mother did each day, but if she thought to ask Sabine was assured there was lots for her mother to do – her support of her husband's career and her role as patron of various charities was such a full-time commitment that there was no time for a career of her own. It wasn't until Sabine was a teenager that she became aware of her mother's previous life as a ballet dancer. Learnt not from her parents, but as a result of overhearing chit chat from various visitors. Chit chat along the lines of: *You'd think she'd miss it – all that fame and adulation. To leave that – for this?* Not that *this* was too shabby – a harbourside residence in a prestige Sydney suburb, marriage to one of the pre-eminent legal minds of the century as he was so often described and a life of ease and comfort. Yet sometimes Sabine wondered if the serene presence that her mother displayed to the world was in fact an enigmatic mask that very rarely was let slip. Anna was her mother and should have been an open book to her daughter, but there was so much about her that was unknown.

Today however her mother behaved as she always had. Smiling calmly as she graciously accepted the words of condolence that were murmured in her ear, together with the kisses, hugs and pats that were loaded onto her. Sabine had tried her best to be the supportive daughter, but soon she found it all too much to bear. Keeping a wary eye on her uncle whom she knew from past experience would be monitoring the crowd with the intent to police bad behaviour, she eased her way to the side wall as if seeking refreshment, smiling and exchanging brief conversation with people who seemed to know her, but as far as she was concerned were total strangers.

Destination reached, and as she fussed over pouring tea and adding a splash of milk Sabine considered her options. She had had enough. Her mother didn't need her – really when had she ever needed her? And anyway, her uncle would easily take charge, like he always did when her father was not around. With a feeling of dread she wondered if that would be their experience every day from now on. That her uncle would step in and take over their lives. A situation she could not bring herself to contemplate. All Sabine wanted to do was retreat to the safety of her home, to take her time to contemplate the events of the last week and try to make some sense of it. There was no need to go to work today or indeed for the rest of the week. That was the advantage of working for a major law firm. The death of her father they took as a loss, not just to his family, but also to the entire legal community. Her boss had insisted she take time off when really all she wanted to do was bury herself in her work by way of distraction from the thoughts that kept circling in her head. At least she could get out of here and maybe go home and take the dog to the beach for a run or something. The need to do something physical was almost an ache that if not assuaged would very soon send her into hysterics. She didn't know how her mother over there could be so polite to these no doubt well-meaning strangers. All she wanted to do was to get away as far as possible and as soon as she could.

Putting the undrunk cup of tea on the table she turned and surreptitiously headed to the side door. But not quick enough. A hand grabbed her arm, bringing Sabine to a halt.

'There you are. Sabine, I'm not sure if you remember me?'

A younger voice this time. Not like the older voices that had been murmuring their condolences one after the other until all she wanted to do was scream. A deep clear-cut voice and a firm strong grip on her arm. A smell like warm toast or hay – outdoorsy and unexpectedly comforting. She turned and contemplated the man standing beside her. A stranger – but a handsome one, attired in the dark grey pinstripe suit so beloved by lawyers.

'No. I don't think I do. Have we met before?'

'Only in passing. I worked for your father a few years ago as his associate before I went to the bar.' His hand now removed from her arm was held out as if to initiate a handshake.

'Max Sumner. I'm so pleased to meet again, even if it's on such a sad occasion. Your dad was a great man and a great lawyer, but I suppose you've heard that so many times already today?' His eyes crinkly as he smiled at her. The warmth and empathy radiating from him somehow infiltrated Sabine's mood and despite her best intentions of fleeing she found herself wanting to find out more about this man whom she was meant to have met before.

'Yes of course. We would most certainly have met before if you worked for my father but I'm finding this all a bit overwhelming today. Too many people and too many faces. Even at the best of times I'm not great at remembering faces but today...', her voice trailed off as Sabine forced her face muscles to contort into what she hoped was the semblance of a smile.

He smiled that smile again. She felt a need to prolong contact as if she could draw on his energy and give herself the strength to continue. But not here. This place was just doing her head in.

'Tell you what. I could kill for a decent coffee. Do you want to join me at the café down the road? I think the coffee there is adequate and I really do need to get away.'

'Your mum?'

'She's fine. My uncle is taking good care of her. She won't even know I'm gone.'

Shoulder by shoulder they contemplated Anna, standing across the other side of the room, and hovering by her side the bulk of Sabine's uncle who as ever was solicitous as he murmured what Sabine could only hope were words of comfort into her mother's ear.

No, she wouldn't miss her at all.

'Quick. Out the side door.'

Sometime later in a deserted café and while sipping cappuccinos that were surprisingly good, they took their time to get to know each other. Sabine, if she was honest with herself still couldn't remember ever having met this Max before but then again, she never paid much notice to the eager young legal graduates who spent the first twelve months of their career as an associate for her father. She knew it was considered a prestigious position to have on a lawyer's CV but for some reason she had never been interested in applying for that role. Sabine tried to explain this to her coffee companion.

'No, I was never interested in being a judge's associate for my father or for anyone else for that matter. Even though dad did occasionally encourage me to join him. I think he liked the idea of his daughter assisting him with his work and his decisions – you know, a sort of dynastic thing. But the thought of sitting in a courtroom all day was so not for me. There's no way I could sit still for that long.' Sabine grimaced in disgust. 'But what about you? Did you enjoy it?'

'Sort of. To start with it was very strange. So different to law school. It was like entering into a whole new world. Like joining a secret society. All that protocol and rules of procedure that they never teach you in legal studies. I always knew I wanted to become a barrister, so it seemed to me a quick way of learning the ropes – seeing it from the other side so to speak. And your father was a great boss – so informative and kind.'

'Was he?' Sabine asked, her forehead wrinkling, feeling perplexed. These were not the words Sabine felt she could apply to the father she knew – the man who was forever urging her to excel at whatever she did. A man who was so competitive with everyone – even his daughter.

'He certainly was. He encouraged me to go to the Bar – said that I had the potential to get to the *top of the tree* – whatever that was. You know I really looked up to him – none of my family went to university so I often felt out of my depth. Without his encouragement I don't know where I would have ended up.'

Looking directly at Sabine Max continued: 'He often spoke of you – how proud he was of you and what you were achieving.'

'Really? That's all news to me!'

'Believe me. He did and the last time I saw him – at an official drinks event – start of the legal year you know? It was only the other week. We got talking. He said you were now with a top tier law firm – *Smithtons* isn't it? He was pretty keen on us to meet as he thought we would have lots in common. But sadly, that never had a chance to happen.'

Now that was not what she wanted to hear. Another example of her father trying to set her up with a *suitable young man* from a *good family*. Or someone he considered had prospects that would make them suitable to become part of the Judge's family. Even from beyond the grave it appeared that her father was still at it. No matter how easy on the eye and how well this man smelt she was not going to get involved with anyone who was chosen by another for her. The expression on her face must have given some clue to Sabine's thoughts as Max, reached out to touch her arm, and spoke again:

'Sorry. That came out all wrong. All I wanted to say was that I really admired your father and I am pleased we could finally meet. I'm so sorry for you and your mother and I hope in time you could bring yourself to catch up with me again. Nothing too complicated. Just a chance to get to know each other. Maybe go to the beach or a walk or something? Can I give you my phone number?'

How could she refuse? Taking his number didn't mean a lifetime commitment. Anyway, looking at his earnest expression there seemed no reason to suspect he was other than sincere.

\*\*\*

By the time she reached home it was late – too late to brave the traffic to take the dog to the beach. A walk in the nearby park would just have to do. Stella her flatmate was already home from work and was eager to find out how the day went.

'You could do with a walk too Stella,' said Sabine as she pushed the excited jumping ball of fluff to the ground. 'Grover, give up. Just settle. We'll go as soon as I find your lead and we definitely will drag this lazy woman with us. Come on Stella, don't be a slacker!'

'All right, all right.' The other woman raised her hands in mock surrender, her cheeky grin giving lie to her words. 'Let me find some walking shoes and I'll be right there.'

The closest park was some two blocks away – a short walk that entailed meandering around back lanes lined with creative graffiti and littered with rubbish, then crossing one very busy road. Once there and contrary to the signs that dotted the perimeter, they let the dog off the lead and slowly followed him as he raced along some haphazard path that was predetermined by his tiny brain – racing from scent to scent. Stella and Sabine in lock step initially were silent until Stella spoke up:

'How did it go?'

No need to explain what *it* was.

'Awful. The chapel was full of important people – totally full and overflowing. Most of them I barely knew – if at all. The service was so, so very long – all about the judge and his career and not about the man, you know the real person who was my father and mum's husband. Although now that I come to think about it, I'm beginning to wonder if any of us really knew much about who that man really was,' Sabine said thoughtfully. 'He was a mystery – not that I was ever concerned about that. I thought he would be in my life for much longer and that in time I might get to know him properly,' she said and then added, 'or maybe not.'

'And your mum?'

Sabine shrugged.

'Who knows. She was keeping everything to herself as usual. My uncle was monitoring her every move. If he ever needs a new job, he would be a shoe in as a security guard. You should have seen him – vetting everyone that came near her and moving some of them on. Almost as if he didn't approve of them. Yet mum didn't seem to notice. It was like she was on some other planet – like it was a cardboard cut-out of her. I don't think she even noticed when I left.'

'You left early?'

'Yeah. I went and had a coffee with some guy that once worked for dad.'

With her head to one side, Sabine once more reviewed the brief interlude with Max. 'You know he kind of seemed kind of OK. Not too stuffy – and now I think about it maybe not one of those private school sorts we usually meet – he said something about being the first in his family to go through uni. Yet it didn't seem right to talk to him today – being dad's funeral and all. But we did exchange phone numbers and he seemed keen to see me again.'

Stella jabbed her in the ribs and with a smirk said:

'Grab them when you see them I say. Not much hetero talent on the ground in this city.'

Then with a serious look.

'Should you go back to your home tonight?'

'No. I couldn't bear it. I know it's going to take some time, but I dread going back. Everywhere I look I would see my father. It's too soon. Maybe I can meet mum somewhere? Some place that is neutral ground – somewhere that dad has never been. I think I could manage that. Maybe here? She could help me walk the dog – that is if we can find him? Where has he gone this time? Grover? GROVER! Leave that other dog alone!'

# Chapter Three

# The next day - Anna and Sabine

'Really Sabine. There was no need to come over and drag me out. I have more than enough to do. Besides which shouldn't you be at work?'

'No ma. I told you already. Work has given me leave for the rest of this week. I don't need to go back until Monday. I thought you might need to get away from home for a break. It's just on lunchtime and I'm starving. Fancy going somewhere to eat? Maybe later on we could drop by my place and you could walk the dog with me?' Sabine looked at her mother hopefully. Any excuse for lunch worked for her and now that she had the opportunity to look closely at her mother, she suspected that eating had been a low priority since her husband had died.

'Very well,' her mother conceded defeat. 'But I totally refuse to walk that dog. He's too jumpy and I have no interest in chasing him around a park. Have you thought about obedience training?'

'Ma. Of course, I did! Not only did I think of it, but Grover and I attended those classes several times and each time he was kicked out for bad behaviour. He's a disgrace to his breed.'

'And what breed would that be?' her mother asked in dulcet tones knowing full well he was a stray of uncertain parentage.

'Never mind that,' Sabine was not going to concede her dog's mysterious pedigree. 'Let's do lunch then. I could eat a banquet.

But how about we go to Watson's Bay? Fish and chips? And maybe a paddle?' said with what she hoped was an enticing smile.

Somehow it worked. Her mother's expression lightened with a faint smile and for a moment it was possible to see the charm that had once shone through, before sorrow and sleepless nights had left their mark on her face. Taking only a moment to locate her handbag Anna was ready to follow her daughter who was already impatiently striding down the garden path towards the car jangling car keys, all the while chattering about something. Something incomprehensible to her mother as Sabine was more or less out of earshot. As always Sabine was in a rush, heedless of the fact that her mother had yet to lock the front door or to catch up.

The drive to Watson's Bay was its usual congested journey, but for once Anna didn't mind. She let Sabine's chatter wash over her, occasionally giving a murmured grunt to indicate she was paying attention but in reality it was all background noise to her. She was accustomed to how her daughter seemed to have an endless supply of conversation. In fact, Anna was convinced Sabine had been born full of chatter. From the initial squawk of protest upon her rushed arrival into the world it seemed to Anna that the only time her daughter was quiet was when she was asleep. Sometimes this could be a trial for a woman who enjoyed solitude however, on this occasion, it was a welcome distraction. She would never admit it to her daughter but leaving the house today had been a good idea. Not something that she could have initiated and for once she was grateful to her pushy daughter for insisting on this outing.

The day was sunny and humid. The air thick with moisture and the promise of an afternoon storm. She gazed out the car window taking in the fleeting glimpses of the harbour and admired the variety of dwellings large and small that lined the streets through which they travelled. Eventually reaching Watson's Bay they took some time to locate a vacant parking space, but finally success was theirs just as it was time for lunch. A leisurely stroll along the street brought them to the café that flanked the harbour. They were in luck as a table with a view along the sandy shoreline and across the water was quickly found for them.

The fish and chips were as delicious as they had expected and in between mouthfuls Sabine kept up a flow of constant chatter - whether from nerves or from a need to talk about anything other than recent events was not apparent. Her mother, having discovered that she was hungry after all focussed on eating silently and intently and let her daughter carry on. Such behaviour was a common occurrence after all. But there was a limit. Holding up her hand she halted Sabine in mid-flow concerning some work anecdote about people Anna had never met, as she interrupted:

'Enough my dear. Your lunch is going cold, and I really don't need to know any more about the goings on of your colleagues – fascinating though they may be. It's lovely you are here with me today and I really appreciate you taking time to see me – but maybe if we have to talk do you think we could discuss matters closer to home?'

An apprehensive look crossed Sabine's face. She was unaccustomed to her mother taking the initiative. In the not too distant past, it had always been her father who directed the conversation. Sabine suspected that in his absence her mother now felt the need to step in and take over control. At her mother's words she fell silent and waited. Maybe things might be different in this strange new world absent a male head of family.

Anna smiled gently at her only child and as if she could read her daughter's mind continued:

'It's ok to admit we have now arrived in a strange new world. A place without your father in it. To be honest I still cannot imagine an existence where I wake up every morning on my own and I'm still struggling with trying to imagine a future that doesn't have your father in it. I suppose it is early days and I cannot rush things but...'

At this Anna paused, put down her knife and fork which she had been clutching and rested her hands on the table, as if trying to gain reassurance from the stolid inanimate timber that neither resisted nor surrendered to her touch.

'I accept that death has to happen to us all. It's just I never thought...' her voice trailed off as Anna struggled to find the right words and then she continued in a soft voice, almost as if she was speaking to herself. 'I suppose I feel like the rug has been pulled out from under me. As if the world I knew has disappeared down some sort of sink hole. I suppose that's how someone who has just experienced a natural disaster might feel when their home is destroyed by earthquake or fire. I realise I should be grateful I still have my home, have you and the security of your father's pension, but at the moment I feel numb. Like I am nothing and no-one. I mean what will I do now?'

Anna looked at her daughter. Her expression was almost pleading – as if she thought her daughter would have the answer. As if Sabine would step into her father's shoes and direct Anna just like he had always done. With as much compassion as she could she returned her mother's gaze. It dawned on Sabine that she had no idea how to help. Other than to grasp both Anna's hands in her much larger ones and try to give comfort. This she did and to an extent it seemed to be what Anna was currently looking for – reassurance that she was not alone.

'There, there, ma. We're in this together, remember? You are so not alone. Neither of us had any inkling he was unwell, and I suspect neither did he. I'm sure Dad is presently looking down at us all the while carrying on about how he hadn't finished his work and how he needs to get back to the job. I can just imagine dad saying he didn't have any spare time for this dying caper, and didn't anyone see he had a judgement to complete? You can just visualise him telling the Grim Reaper to bugger off!'

A muffled unladylike snort from her mother greeted Sabine's words.

'And you can just pity the poor sod who has been tasked with taking over the matter dad was working on that afternoon when he died and having to review the transcript with a hope of reaching a decision. If Dad will be haunting anyone it will be that person. I can just imagine Dad peering over his shoulder as the poor judge reviews the proceedings – blowing cold in his or her ear if they dare to reach a conclusion that differs from how dad thought the case should go!'

Her mum laughed and as she wiped tears from her eyes.

'Oh Sabine. I really needed your humour. The last few days with all that sympathy and kind words has almost brought me undone. Of course, it is lovely that people care but I wish they would just leave me alone. But not you.' With a marked change of tone that indicated it was time to discuss business she continued: 'I know it's early days, but there are matters that must be attended to and I would appreciate you being there with me – if only to keep me from falling apart.'

'Matters?'

'Yes. There's your father's clothing for starters. That should be fairly straightforward. I suppose it can all be donated to some charity shop. I won't need your help with that task. But there is also the matter of his legal books and whatever he kept in his study and at his chambers. I can't go through that on my own....... Maybe you will help me? If you can?'

Sabine felt her innards clench as she contemplated venturing into the inner sanctum that was her father's study and also into his legal chambers. As a child she was never permitted entry and even as an adult these were places that were kept for her father's exclusive use. But what choice did she have when faced with her mother's pleading eyes? For she knew that if access had been denied to her, it had also been prohibited to her mother. Somehow the two of them must find the courage to storm the judge's domain. With a shrug Sabine acknowledged defeat.

'Of course. Whenever you want me to help, I'll be there. I suppose clearing out his chambers must be the priority as they will be needed for Dad's replacement, who I expect will be appointed soon. Just tell me when and I'll meet you there,' she said with what she hoped was a look of confidence and an indication that it would not be a big deal.

Yet somehow, she thought it might.

# Chapter Four

# The Judge's Chambers

Only through the exercise of will and the strategic use of an alarm clock did Sabine manage to meet her mother in town at the agreed time. Getting dressed had been a rushed job and as she greeted her mother with a kiss, she was conscious of the critical assessment of her appearance by her mother. Once again Sabine felt she had been found lacking.

'Sorry ma. I slept in. A bit of a rush to get here in time, but then again it doesn't matter what I look like today. Surely?' Sabine glanced down at her outfit of jeans and tank top worn under an unbuttoned floral cotton cardigan, which she had considered acceptable that morning, but on second thoughts, now looked decidedly scruffy when compared to her mother's attire of tailored trousers, blue and white striped buttoned shirt and a triple strand of cultured pearls. Sabine's outfit was more beach attire than city wear. Too bad she thought, giving a mental shrug. As if anyone would notice her when her mother was present, she might as well be invisible.

The judges' chambers were located in the city's business district in the same building as the court rooms, but on a separate floor. First there was the security to be negotiated and then a lengthy wait while they waited for the judge's current associate to be located and fetched to escort them. When he arrived, he looked to Sabine like all the other associates who had worked for her father. A generic lawyer: he was well groomed – with short hair, no beard – no surprise there, as she was well aware that her father did not approve of facial hair. And dressed in the usual legal uniform of charcoal grey pin-striped suit. A male of course. As far as Sabine could recall her father had never employed a female associate.

Polite, well-spoken, and immediately forgettable the young man uttered the usual condolences to her mother and with a wave escorted them through further security and then via the lift to the correct floor. He led them down a corridor from which identical wooden doors opened. Stopping at a door indistinguishable from all the others he paused and with a chirpy *Here we are,* he opened it with a flourish. They entered a small room furnished with two wooden desks one of which she assumed was his and at the other sat a woman, focused on her typing. Upon seeing them enter she jumped up and launched herself at Sabine's mother all the while uttering an endless stream of sorrow for the family's loss and with tears shared her own sorrow about the loss of the *perfect boss*. Sabine could only assume, this woman must be her father's secretary, the woman she had often heard her father speak of dismissively but had never met.

The young man was clearly used to the behaviour of this woman and stood by impassively waiting for the emotional torrent to end. Anna remained frozen as she submitted to the woman's embrace and then, with a gentle pat on her back managed somehow to extricate herself giving murmured excuses and moved to the door at the rear of the room.

'Through here then?' she asked the young man, as she paused by the heavily timbered door. He nodded. Following in Anna's footsteps, he reached across and opened the door into an enormous room and waved them through.

'I'll leave you here. The legal books lining the shelves by and large will stay, but there are a few books which I have identified as belonging to the judge – see over there.' He waved a hand in a sweeping movement. 'I have left them on this side table. His personal belongings are still where he kept them – on the desk and in the drawers. There are some bits and pieces in that cupboard there and over on that bureau. If you would please place what you want to take in those boxes over there, I will arrange to have them delivered to your home Mrs Faulkner. I'll leave you now but if you need me, I'll be right next door at my desk. Just call if you need any assistance.'

Sabine was barely conscious of her mother responding to this young man with a few questions of her own concerning arrangements. Standing just inside the doorway Sabine took a moment to look around and consider the furnishings. So this then was her father's work place. The chambers of the oh so important judge of the Supreme Court. There at that antique mahogany desk was where he worked on his insightful decisions which, more often than not, were affirmed on appeal to a higher court. On the odd occasion his decision was overturned it was as if a cataclysmic injustice had taken place His deeply felt righteous indignation accompanied by so much venting and outrage that someone else thought they knew better than him. If this had been the behaviour of a stranger, she might have found it amusing, but as it was her father behaving so, Sabine found it downright embarrassing. At least she could be relieved that such occasions rarely occurred.

In a corner, away from the desk four tub chairs faced each other across a glass coffee table and lining every available space were bookcases crammed with what appeared to be legal publications. The window which looked out across the road to another building was screened with a sheer blind. Nothing to see out there. Anything of note took place inside this room and inside the learned judge's brain.

Once the young man closed the door Sabine turned to her mother, who like her, was standing still – only her head moved as she silently took in the details of the room.

'OK Ma where do you want to start? Will we box his books? Or at least those books we think are his? It's going to be a bit of guesswork, as I've never been here before. Have you?'

'No. Never. Your father kept his work to himself. I suppose he had his reasons, but I never thought to ask. He even kept his study at home locked when he wasn't in it.' Anna shook her head as if displacing such thoughts.

'Still now is not the time to be worrying about that. The sooner we get going, the sooner we can get out of here, and never come back. I'll start on this bureau here – it's largely photos and what look like souvenirs. You do the desk drawers. Rubbish in the bin and anything worth keeping in that box there.'

The top drawer was easy – pens, pencils and brightly coloured post-it notes that by their very colours seemed to be a most surprising choice for the conservative man that had been her father. Pushed to the back Sabine found a hand-held dictating machine. The judge after all was a man of a certain age who did not believe in doing his own typing. The next drawer contained several ruled yellow legal note pads, a bundle of old bank statements and what looked to be a number of business cards that had appeared to have been thrown in haphazardly.

The bottom, much deeper drawer – was locked and did not respond to her frantic tugging. A search for the key on the mess scattered over the top of the desk, and in the other open drawer was unsuccessful. With a sigh she admitted defeat and then called to her mother who seemed to have settled into a chair while she thumbed through a book that appeared to be the latest crime best seller.

'Ma, this bottom drawer is locked. I can't find the key. The desk looks too good to smash. What should I do?'

Her mother almost reluctantly put down the novel and then reached into her handbag.

'Here. Try your father's keys. Luckily, I thought to bring them – just in case they were needed. If the key isn't here, then I guess we will have to call in the locksmith.'

The keyring, a clutch of many keys was quite a weight. Sabine examined the individual keys. Some she could identify as the key to his car and the house key but the others were a mystery. There were at least four smaller keys that could be desk keys – either for his chambers or for his home office. The only way to find out was to start to try them one by one – a bit like trying on the glass slipper from one of her favourite childhood fairy tales. No luck with the first key. It was too large for the lock. The second key did fit but wouldn't turn, but the third – just like in any fairy tale was *just right* and with a smooth turn, the lock gave way, and she was able to ease the drawer open.

She was not sure what she was expecting to find. After all if her father had gone to the trouble of locking this drawer, surely the contents should be extremely valuable? Cash, jewellery, love letters or something else that must be kept secure? But all she could see was a battered folder tied up with the pink tape so beloved of legal firms many years ago. Her first thought was that it couldn't be her father's will, for that had already been located and was now in the possession of the family solicitor. So, what could it be?

She lifted the folder out and placed it gently on the desk in front of her. With a wary eye on her mother, who she could see had abandoned her sorting task and was now curled up in the tub chair, absorbed in the novel, Sabine carefully untied the faded pink tape and then opened the folder. To her bemusement the folder contained no legal documents. Instead there appeared to be a bundle of faded newspaper and magazine clippings and some neatly folded correspondence.

The clippings she spread out before her and read – and reread. All of them told the same story – of how a young Anna Leon was giving up fame and fortune for love. Each article accompanied by a photo of a young Anna, ballerina with a glittering career ahead of her. Photos of Anna *en pointe* with arms gracefully above her head or performing a *pas des deux* with her favourite dance partner, who as one article speculated had for so long been thought to be her romantic partner. A young woman with black hair sleekly styled in a bun, with large almond shaped eyes enhanced with dark eye makeup and whose beauty even now shone through in these faded images. That young woman Sabine recognised. For she was the woman who had become her mother and had never danced again. But why?

There were only a few letters. Sabine hesitated. Maybe she shouldn't open them? After all they belonged to someone else, and Sabine knew she really shouldn't intrude on another's personal affairs. But with a side glance at her mother who was still lost in whatever she was reading, Sabine thought as she often did before diving into yet another ill-thought-out escapade – *Why not?* Finding no satisfactory answer, she opened the first letter.

It was addressed to her father and appeared to be from someone called Andre. Sabine assumed this person called Andre might be her mother's former dance partner for that was the name he was referred to in the articles she had just perused. The letter was short and to the point:

*Antony,*

*Anna deserves so much better than you. I cannot believe you would entice her to abandon her gift for dance and sacrifice so much just to pander to you. And how could you convince her to walk away from her obligations to me and to the company. Believe me you will pay for this treachery one day.*

*I'm sure she will regret her decision and I promise you I will be there to pick up the pieces when the time comes. For she will be unhappy. There's no doubt about that. You cannot care for her and her talents like I and the company do.*

*I spoke to her last night and she assures me that her mind is made up. I don't know what you did to persuade her to give up so much that is part of her. But against my better instincts I have promised Anna I will let her go and not stand in her way. So, you have my word that I will keep away from Anna and not interfere. But believe me if at any time I consider I need to make contact with her I will not hesitate to do so.*

*I cannot say that I send you my best wishes, but I suppose that in your own way you believe you are doing what is best for my beautiful girl.*

*Andre*

There was no other letter from this Andre person in the small bundle of letters. Presumably he had kept his undertaking not to make further contact with Anna, for as far as Sabine could recall, she had never met anyone of that name. The other correspondence appeared to be short handwritten notes of congratulations on the birth of a daughter. Notes addressed to both Sabine's mother and father yet locked away here in his workplace. But why? The only person who could help her was currently a million miles away engrossed in whatever story was contained in the book held tightly by expertly manicured hands. Nothing for it, Sabine needed to know.

'Ma. Look what I have found. What's this about?'

Her mother looked up and for a moment it was clear her thoughts were on another time and place. Then with a shake of her head, Anna's eyes came into focus as she gazed thoughtfully at her daughter looking so regal — well scruffily regal, behind the enormous desk. With a smile she contemplated her daughter looking just like she could, one day be right at home behind such a desk in a judge's chambers. Sabine could tell exactly what her mother was thinking.

'No way Ma. No judge profession for me. Forget it. In fact, there are some days I am not even sure I am meant to be a lawyer and now that Dad is dead, I can say that without giving him apoplexy' Sabina softened her comment with a smile. 'Anyway, look at this folder and tell me what it's all about.'

In one graceful movement her mother uncurled, arose then glided across to the desk. She sat down at the spare chair facing Sabine and reached for the folder into which Sabine had returned the documents.

It took her a while to read and reread the documents. All the while Sabine tried to be patient — but patience was a stranger to her personality, something admired in others but seriously lacking in her character. Standing up she strode around the room and every so often glancing across at her mother who, reading now complete, sat still as she gazed at the open folder in her lap.

'Well?' asked Sabine.

'Well, what my dear,' her mother responded with a weak smile.

'What's that all about? Why did he lock all that away?'

With a sigh her mother seemed to accept she owed her daughter an explanation.

'I suppose he didn't want me to find these papers. Perhaps that's why they weren't kept at home. Mind you the newspaper extracts and magazine articles, I suppose would be easy to find on the Internet if I could ever have bothered. But the rest is all new to me. Like this letter from Andre. I've never seen that before, but it comes as no surprise. Andre just couldn't understand why I behaved as I did all those years ago. And your father had no time for him. Chalk and cheese, they were. These other letters were sent when you were born. I wish I'd seen them then.'

'But why? Why would he keep them from you?'

'Your father was a complex man. So much of him and why he behaved as he did was a mystery to me. I can only imagine he must have had his reasons, but to be honest I cannot fathom what this is all about. I can guess, but it will be a long story.'

'So tell me.'

# Chapter Five

# Anna the Ballerina

Once upon a time there was a little girl and all that young girl wanted to do was dance. From the moment she could walk she walked on her tip toes with arms fluttering as she moved to the rhythm of the music that sounded in her head. That little girl was Anna Leon. No middle name – just Anna and she lived in country NSW. Not a good start for a budding ballerina when the only dance school was a good hour's drive down a dusty dirt road to the nearest town. However, she was gifted with the support of a loving mother who recognised that her daughter was destined for a life far away from the family farm and one not involving years of toil and premature aging as a farmer's wife.

A dance school in the nearby town was located and Anna was enrolled from the age of 4. Perhaps she was enrolled at such a young age in the forlorn hope that she would lose interest and move onto some farm compatible interest. But that was not to be. With each year her interest and her ability grew. A weekly dance lesson morphed into twice a week and then three times a week. In the school holidays she would help the ballet mistress with the classes for the little ones. For this lady had recognised Anna's talent and along with her mother, did all she could to develop this young girl's dancing ability.

To her father this fixation on dance was incomprehensible. Such interests were alien to his everyday activities, where considerations of stock numbers, stock feed and adequate drinking water reigned supreme. But he loved his little girl and glowed with pride each time he watched her perform at the dance school annual concert. Her mother bore the burden of transporting her daughter to and from dance school – maybe not with delight, but at the least with acceptance that perhaps this talent might lead her child away from the only other available options in this small town – early motherhood and a lifetime of making do.

It was Mrs Mac the dance teacher who encouraged Anna to try out for the special intensive programme held by the Classical Ballet School in Melbourne scheduled to be held during the school holidays. A video of her dancing was sent off and, on a day that she would forever remember, notification was received in the mail of her acceptance into the programme. This was the start of Anna's gradual move away from home and towards a new life. For some time, her participation was confined to the school holiday programme until one day when she was 15, her parents accepted the inevitable and applied for her to study full time at the ballet school.

Her talent and commitment paid off over subsequent years and upon graduation Anna was offered a place in the Corps de Ballet. And the rest, as they say, is history. Or as Anna, now telling her daughter said – was *past history*.

'It was all so long ago. Almost like it was another life and happening to another person. I find those times so hard to recall.'

'Yet ma you must have loved it and look,' gesturing at the newspaper extracts now lying on the desk in front of Anna. 'All these articles go on about how talented you were. How could you walk away from that – it was your life!'

'At the time I felt like dancing and being your father's wife were mutually exclusive. You know I thought that I couldn't do both to the standard I would want. To be a ballerina I had to give it my all – every day involved practice and a complete commitment to the craft – body and soul. There would have been no room for anything else – certainly no room for your father. And he was not the sort to stand in line and be second best. So, I made my choice, and at the time it was a choice I was prepared to make. I was so in love and to be honest I also had a number of nagging injuries. The idea of taking a spell from dance was at the time an attractive one. It's just …. It is just I never thought that it would be forever,' Anna's voice trailed off as she contemplated her past.

'Why didn't you go back? Even in some minor way that didn't demand absolute commitment – surely something like that could have been possible?'

Her mother smiled lovingly across at this daughter of hers who only saw things in black and white and had yet to understand that sometimes life was not so simple.

'It's complicated. Yes, my body did recover in time with rest, regular massage and physio. It probably helped that I always was diligent with my stretches and exercises each morning. Maybe I did consider returning. It's so long ago I'm now not sure what was going through my mind at that time. But then you came along. Your father was still practising as a barrister, and his working hours were such that he couldn't be a hands-on dad. So, you took up a lot of my time. And I was happy to be a mum – you were such a delight – and I might add such a challenge. Keeping track of you always kept me on my toes! You could disappear in an instant – worse than that dog of yours for running away. And then as you got older and I got involved in all my charity work, it was like there was no time and I was so much older by then. Probably too old by then. Also, to be a ballerina is an overwhelming undertaking – a hundred percent commitment and I suspect it was a commitment that I lacked. Or maybe because I couldn't see how I could juggle career, baby and be a support to your father. You see to be a ballerina is an absolute vocation. The harsh physical reality of the extent of the work involved in preparing my body for performance at an elite level is hard to understand if you haven't been there. I did try to be realistic and accept that it was a case of either the ballet or a life with your father and then you -it couldn't be both and of course it is obvious what I then chose.'

Sabine closely considered her mother and noted the tensely clasped hands in her lap in stark contrast to her mother's calm face – her expression as usual giving no clue as to her feelings.

'And now?'

'Now?'

'Well dad is dead. The charities and all the stuff you did to support him – surely that can be ditched if you want?'

'Maybe…. I don't know.' Her mother frowned then shook her head. 'It's too soon. You're asking me to make plans for my future when I have yet to work through all this', her left hand gestured to the remnants of her husband's life that were still scattered around the room.

'Too soon Sabine. Way too soon. Give me time.'

'Well at the very least will you get in touch with these people who once cared enough to write to you? Or even just Andre?'

'Maybe.' She said in a tone of voice that indicated the conversation was over – for now. But Sabine had never been deterred so easily. She knew what she had to do.

# Chapter Six

## Sabine the young lawyer

First day back at work on Monday was strange. It was a little over two weeks since her father had died. Time since his death had been swept up into the vortex of grief. Time counted in days that had passed and yet in some ways it felt like months or even years had elapsed. The life Sabine had lived before was no longer – taking her parents for granted and with complete disinterest in their life and feelings now seemed like a very selfish approach. She found herself regretting that she had never made the effort to challenge her father – to find out who he really was and what he thought. Her past behaviour of ignoring her father's pronouncements or diatribes, not disputing them or at the very least trying to clarify them seemed, on fresh consideration to be self-centred. Had Sabine been so focused on herself that she never wondered why her father thought as he did?

So much about her parents was a mystery. Why had her mother walked away from fame and a career that she loved with such a passion for a marriage with someone who had as far as Sabine could tell, no shared background or common interests? Why did it have to be either or – ballet or marriage? Was this at her father's insistence? She knew that her father always wanted to get his own way and if this didn't occur then there would be a massive sulk or temper tantrum. Once seen always to be avoided. Maybe this was also how her mother felt? Not that she would ever share this with her daughter. That was not her mother's way. Private to the very end. Still there was this mysterious Andre. Maybe she could track him down? These days no one would remain hidden for long thanks to the Internet and all the various sites that she could access.

Keen as she was to get sleuthing Sabine knew that first she had to survive a day at work. The sympathy from her colleagues set her teeth on edge but she managed to smile sweetly each time someone trotted out the usual condolences and tried her hardest not to snap back at them.

It was a relief to be summonsed to see her supervising partner – her boss. Sabine as a recent law graduate had only been with the law firm for two months and was still concerned about what was appropriate behaviour when in the presence of a partner of the firm. *Smithtons* was one of the so-called *top tier* law firms in Sydney. A firm that had been in existence for over one hundred years with a stable of clients that read like the *Who's Who* of the Australian business world. It was a privilege to be employed by this firm as she had heard so many times from friends and family since she had received the job offer. To work at the top of the top with the best lawyers in Australia was something she should treasure, or so she had been told, as being employed here implied that she too, was one of the best. If only she didn't have this nagging doubt that this law firm was not the place for her. To not be happy in her employment at *Smithtons* smacked of ingratitude, when it was considered to be one of the most desired legal jobs in Sydney. Sabine told herself to be patient – it was early days after all and as she had been told at her induction, she would be given the opportunity in her graduate year to sample all the types of legal challenges that legal practice at *Smithtons* would offer, with a view to her then being able to apply for the work area that most appealed when her graduate year had been completed.

The other legal graduates in her intake, all shiny and new, eager to triumph over whatever challenges came their way did not appear to share the same doubts as her. Their obsession with the law reminded Sabine of her father and his single-minded focus on whatever was happening in legal discourse. There was no room in his mind for the distractions of everyday life and listening to the chatter of her colleagues, it seemed like they were cast in exactly the same mould.

Still, she had been fortunate in the allocation of her supervising partner. Rhys Purcell was a junior partner – some 40 years old she thought, but maybe a year or two younger? She was never very good at telling older people's ages. From her not very mature perspective of 24 years everyone over 30 appeared to her to be ancient. With the body of a surfer and a twinkle in his eye he somehow had inveigled his way into a law firm that, in Sabine's opinion was populated mostly by nerds. It probably helped that his major client was one of the largest corporations in the country. She imagined that would give him a degree of influence in any partners' meeting. Yet she still wondered if she was ever going to be brave enough to ask him how he managed to cope with being imprisoned in a metal, glass and concrete tower for more than twelve hours a day. To ask that would give away her own misgivings and her inner voice urged her to keep stum - at least for now.

His greeting when she entered the office was welcoming. No condolences. They had been said before and Rhys was not one given to repetition. Just a *Glad to have you back*, delivered with a welcoming smile and then giving her the reference to an electronic file with the request that she read it and get to work on the first draft of a legal advice to the client setting out a discussion on the initial legal issues and what the recommended next steps would be in resolving the matter.

'This is a fairly straight forward matter – an accident at work. Or advice should consider whether there is any legal liability on the part of the employer or not? Have a look on our intranet for any previous advice we may have given to our clients on similar fact situations, if any. Make sure you have a quick look at the case law and then start drafting our advice – using the format you will find in our precedent system. This shouldn't take long – send me what you have completed by COB today – or first thing tomorrow if you get stuck. OK?'

Sabine could tell that there was no time to object or query the matter. Rhys' attention was already on something else as he swivelled around and peered intently at his computer. Obviously, she had been dismissed. There was nothing for it but to leave. The butterflies in her stomach competing for space as they twirled and fluttered. Her first legal advice for this partner! Nothing for it but to return to her workstation and get started.

Some hours later she stretched and contemplated what she had written. Rhys had been correct. The matter was straightforward. An accident at work involving the failure of machinery which judging by the maintenance log had been inadequately serviced. The injury to the employee was severe, involving trauma and the loss of his right hand which should entitle him to compensation. Although there was the question of whether the employee had himself been careless and contributed to the accident – his blood toxicology indicated a high level of alcohol in his bloodstream. However, there was some confusion about whether he had been drinking in his lunchbreak away from work or whether this was permitted by the employer. Sabine made a note that this would require clarification.

And then there was the question of the investigation by the Work Safe Authority and the potential for a fine to be levied on the employer. All in all, this incident could end up not only being extremely expensive for the organisation but might adversely impact on their reputation and ongoing business profitability.

Her research completed, Sabine turned her attention to drafting the advice, and to her surprise and despite her initial apprehension, she found the words flowed easily. It was just like writing a legal essay after all – but this time it had to be concise and follow the *Smithtons* format. For it had already been explained to her that no client ever wanted to read a legal advice that read like a PhD thesis. How hard can it be she thought? There was nothing to it but to dive right in, just like she did with everything. As she grappled with the challenges of drafting a simple but accurate advice, Sabine lost all track of time until, and with the last word typed, she realised she had done it. Her very first advice now completed. With a rush of exultation at this milestone achievement it took all her will not to leap up pumping the air with enthusiasm. This was an open plan office after all. She leant back in her chair, stretched and looked around. A young woman at a neighbouring workstation looked up and smiled.

'At last, you return to the land of the living. I thought you had been sucked into some legal other world. You have been so intent on your computer for hours.'

'Sorry. It's just that it's my first advice for Rhys and I was terrified of stuffing it up. And come to think of it, I still am. Maybe some time away from my desk would help clear my mind, before I do a final review and send it off to the boss. A walk perhaps. Want to join me?'

'Sure. Let me change my shoes and we can do a bit of power walking.'

A short while later, both now wearing their trainers which looked rather incongruous when worn with black shift dresses, they set off up Bridge Street in the direction of the Botanic Gardens.

Amy who was Sabine's workstation neighbour was also part of the graduate intake and like Sabine, had been preoccupied that day working to a deadline, researching something she had never done before. As they strode along, dodging other pedestrians, they compared notes and shared confidences about how much they dreaded getting anything wrong.

'Do you think it will always be like this? Being asked to do something you've never done before and with a tight deadline? I don't recall this being mentioned at our induction. Maybe it gets easier with time?'

'I certainly hope so!'

They both laughed and continued with the walk. A quick lap around the gardens, a wistful glance at the sparkling harbour tempting them with its spectacular expanse of water and then it was time to get back to the desk, and those looming deadlines.

Later that afternoon Sabine was a silent observer at the weekly conference call with another key client at which Rhys and a senior associate reviewed the matters they were handling for them. The senior associate, an experienced lawyer named Fran Walshe seemed to Sabine to be the sort of lawyer she should aspire to be - friendly, but firm — not in a push over sort of way but strong in a very calm, well-groomed and charming way. Fran was meant to be her supervisor but to date they had had little contact as she had been away from work on maternity leave. Today was her first day back from leave and already Sabine could tell from the discussions, she was about to get to know Fran much better.

'Yes, of course. I and our junior lawyer Sabine Faulkner are working on that matter. We're drafting the Notice of Motion and will run it past you in the next day or so,' said Fran as she smiled significantly at Sabine. And then: 'I'm just getting Sabine to check the case law on such issues and will get back to you shortly with a quick discussion note for you to consider. Say in the next day or so. Will that be alright with you?'

Sabine, frantically scribbling on her notepad could see that there would be no spare time for her. She just hoped that her first draft advice, now completed and sent to Rhys, would be found satisfactory as she could see that would be no time to do anything further on it unless she stayed at work all night.

Conference call ended, she looked up to see both Rhys and Fran grinning at her.

'Welcome to the real world,' Rhys whispered, his face a grin from ear to ear, his teeth on perfect display.

# Chapter Seven

# How the lawyers party - drinks at the Barrister's chambers and afterwards

The rest of the afternoon passed in a blur as Sabine grappled with trying to deliver on what she felt were rather confusing instructions. Several times she resorted to consulting with Amy seeking guidance, but it was not much help for Amy was as confused as her.

It was with some relief when after 5 she saw Fran approach her desk.

'Thank goodness you're here. I'm not sure if I am doing this right. I've done the research you asked me to and I've typed up some key points with reference to where it is supported by case law and/or legislation but I'm not sure how to present it. I was going through the various formats on the system, but I'm stumped by what you mean when you said it would be a *discussion note*. There's no such template labelled on the system.'

'Is that all. If you've got the substance nailed and are only worrying about the formatting, I'm very impressed. Here let me look,' and with that Fran leaned across and scrolled down the page of templates Sabine had open on her computer. Fran pointed at one particular format.

'See, that one will do. But you can finish it off tomorrow. Just save what you have already done and come and join Rhys and me.

We've been invited to the start of legal year drinks up at one of the barristers' chambers. I think at little time out is called for. It's been a long day. Meet us in five out at the lifts. And you too Amy? OK?'

A short time later they were all heading up Martin Place, battling against the tide of commuters who were streaming in the opposite direction, heading for the train and for home. Rhys and Fran were in intense discussion about an issue that had arisen and paid no attention to the people swirling around them. Sabine hung in closely behind accompanied by her workstation neighbour who she now knew was destined to become a close ally.

'So far so good, eh?' Sabine grinned at Amy.

'Well, I'm not so sure – I have been given a heap of work to do and will be in tomorrow early.

Sabine laughed, 'Me too! I think sleeping in is no longer an option!'

They passed the rest of the walk talking about inconsequential things as they got to know each other's background. Sabine didn't mention her father – the grief was too raw for this to be part of general chit chat. She spoke about how she shared an inner-city terrace house with her old university friend Stella in nearby Darlinghurst. She told Amy how she rode her bike to work and the described the number of near misses Sabine had experienced on her daily commute. Amy, it appeared still lived on the North Shore with her family and hoped one day soon to find a place of her own.

'Maybe a bedsit or an apartment nearby so I can walk to work. That would be great.'

'Yeah - and then you will always be in the office or available to come in at short notice!'

By now they had reached the top of Martin Place and were turning right into a street where the barristers' chambers were located not that far from the courts. They entered a multi storey building, up the lift and at a floor selected by Rhys, who clearly knew where he was going, they exited onto a foyer crammed with people and awash with the happy noise of people at play. With excited greetings and waves to people in the crowd Rhys and

Fran were almost immediately subsumed by the crowd leaving two slightly apprehensive young women scanning the crowd for any familiar faces, or if those could not be found then searching out faces that might look slightly welcoming. But all those in the room were busy interacting with each other and paid no mind to the two newcomers.

'Well,' said Sabine drawing a deep breath, 'looks like there is nothing for it than to dive in. There must be someone here we can talk to.'

Amy was not made of such stern stuff, and it was clear by the surreptitious backward steps that all she wanted to do was to retreat. With a sudden grab of her arm by her companion, her attention was diverted.

'Over there. At last I think I've spotted someone I know. Come on.' And Amy surrendering to the propulsion of her workmate allowed herself to be dragged in the direction of a frantically waving woman with wild curly black hair.

'Thank goodness you are here Stella. You're the only one I know in this crowd. Maybe you can introduce us to some others? Anyway, why are you here?'

'Why not? I occasionally brief some of the barristers on this floor and thought it might be good to catch up with a few of them. And a free drink and some nibbles wouldn't go astray – that is if I could find them.'

Stella put out her hand and introduced herself to Amy. Greetings exchanged, and in no time at all connections had been made, common backgrounds exclaimed over and speculation shared as to why they had never met before. A waiter with a drinks tray passed by, then someone with finger food, and they relaxed into further chatter. It wasn't too long until Stella waved enthusiastically at a young man entering the room from the lift.

'Here. Over here Sam.'

A young man of about six foot in height with curly brown hair approached. Dressed casually – jeans, open necked shirt and leather jacket, he stood out in the crowd of dark suits. His grin as he reached them was welcoming, and as he reached in to hug Stella, it was clear they were well acquainted.

'Heya Stella. Great to see you but what are you doing here?'

'I'm getting sick of being asked that. Is it so strange that I might be here?' Her laughing eyes made it clear that no offence was taken and maybe by her tone she was being a little bit flirtatious. 'I brief some of these guys from time to time and I thought it was time I enjoyed some of their hospitality which no doubt I support with the fees that I pay. Here let me introduce you to my friends. Sabine please meet Sam Menzies, a most disreputable man, but a dear friend. Sam, allow me to introduce you to my housemate, Sabine Faulkner. And this is Amy. Sorry I've yet to remember your surname. Amy works with Sabine.'

Sam shook hands with Sabine and stared into her eyes.

'You may not remember me at all Sabine. But I started law with you. However, I only did two years before I decided it wasn't for me. So, I immediately bailed and then transferred to journalism and – hurrah- I found my vocation.'

He grinned as he gestured around the room. 'And my working uniform is so much better than what you lawyers have to wear. I think I got off lightly!'

Sam explained that he now worked for a Sydney newspaper which often covered political and court matters and then reeled off a number of hilarious and slightly scandalous anecdotes to his delighted audience. Sabine found herself examining this person whom she did not recall at all. His height made him stand eye to eye with her, which in her experience was a novelty. Not the tallest person in the room but certainly not the shortest. Brown hair clustered in soft curls on his head and a little longer at the back. Yet to become a mullet, but if left unchecked it soon would be. Eyes of a soft blue that twinkled with good humour, especially now as he played up to his appreciative audience. He looked across at another person approaching their group.

'Ah here's one to watch. A future judge or premier if I'm not mistaken. Heya Max how're things?'

The three young women all turned as one to examine the approaching young man but only Sabine recognised him. It was the young man who had spoken to her at her father's funeral and with whom she had shared a cup of coffee. She recalled how keen he had been to see her again and again felt her reluctance to be acquainted with one of her father's ex-associates. Was she being a snob or was it just that she didn't like him? As he grew close the familiar outdoorsy smell of fresh hay or was it freshly toasted bread assailed her nostrils and she again recalled his kindness on that day not so long ago? Maybe the coincidence of seeing him again so soon signified the start of something, or it could be that as he was a barrister this could be where his chambers are located? She could see both Stella and Amy eyeing him speculatively, and supposed there was no harm in being friendly.

Max in his greetings made it clear that he and Sabine had already met. Sabine was conscious of Stella's questioning gaze but was careful not to give anything away in her response. For a moment she worried that Max might mention the circumstances of their last meeting. There may have been something in her tense expression that indicated this, for Max kept the conversation light and limited to a range of choice legal anecdotes and for this Sabine was grateful. It was obvious Sam and Max were well known to each other and it was easy for Sabine to relax into their banter.

It was sometime later and after several more drinks had been consumed that Stella glancing at her watch and said she needed to leave.

'And probably Beanie you also need to go? That dog of yours won't walk himself!'

'You're right. I'd better go.' And as if hit suddenly by an inspired thought, Sabine smiled, 'We can order some home delivery if you lot want to join us? Nothing fancy but maybe Thai or Chinese from somewhere nearby. You could all organise that while I walk the dog. Good idea?'

Max and Sam were enthusiastic and after taking details of the address promised to join them shortly. Amy with disappointment clear in her expression declined, saying the trip home would take too long if she went to their place. But she then indicated this had made up her mind, the sooner she moved into town the better her social life would be. With reluctant farewells Amy left first while the others made their plans.

The rest of the evening passed as planned. Sabine upon returning home found her beloved dog once more covered in dirt, further excavations having been commenced in the backyard. The unrepentant pooch jumped all over his mistress and then pleased to share with her his delight over his new hobby caused further excitement when he shook the dirt from his shaggy body all over the kitchen floor. Stella entering the room behind Sabine laughed at the mess.

'I'm glad he's your dog and you have to do the cleaning up. Hopefully before you walk him?'

'Of course,' said Sabine reaching for the brush and pan. 'Such a trial you are Grover. I think after today's adventures in the backyard it is clear you need more than a morning and evening walk. Looks like I need to find someone to walk you during the day. There is only so much our backyard can cope with. Already it looks like somewhere from the Somme and once it rains it will be even more so.' As she bent to sweep up the mess the dog sensing a new game with his mistress bounced around her, every so often running forward and licking her on the face.

'Give over you mongrel,' cross words, but said with a laugh so Grover, not speaking the human tongue still understood his mistress was not cross with him. 'Come on, that's done now. Let's get you walked and then fed and maybe – just maybe you might be on your best behaviour by the time our visitors arrive. Stella can I leave it to you to order something for our dinner? I'll eat anything.'

'Don't I know it. I've yet to find something you don't like.'

'Mmmm- maybe liver or black pudding. At a pinch I'll eat them but I'd rather not. Dad always insisted on me eating whatever was on my plate. Lucky for me mum was a good cook and even brussels sprouts cooked by her tasted delectable.'

The rest of the evening passed all too quickly. Dinner was delicious and the company most enjoyable. Max and Sam, who had arrived at the same time bearing bottles of wine and tubs of gourmet ice cream proved to be welcome guests. The house being tiny and lacking a dining room they made do by clustering around a coffee table with various open take away cartons before them. Food was shared and consumed with enthusiasm while supervised by a small dog who tried his hardest to persuade them that he had not eaten for days. It was clear by the way their conversation merged and flowed from shared anecdotes that they had much in common and had indeed spent time together. The fresh company energised Stella and Sabine and they found themselves behaving equally outrageously with the stories they told – tales about colleagues and fellow students from when they were at university as well as anecdotes about a certain dog's outrageous behaviour. Said dog curled up at Sabine's feet looking as if bad behaviour was something he could never contemplate.

Reluctantly Sabine called a halt to the festivities once she noticed the time.

'Hey guys. It's past 11 and I for one am off to bed. I have an early start tomorrow. So much work to do and if I don't get in early tomorrow, I know I'm not going to sleep for the rest of the week because I will be stressing about how I'm going to get it all done. And you all probably have the same. I know I sound a bit like a school marmish, but need I remind you it is a weeknight?'

With smiles and farewells Sam and Max rose to their feet and headed out towards the front door.

'Thanks so much,' said Sam. 'It's been great to see you both again – even if you don't remember me Sabine! Let's do something soon. I often work late but how about next time I have some spare time I will get in touch?'

Sabine and Stella both nodded enthusiastically. Max meanwhile, pulled Stella and then Sabine into a group hug while murmuring his thanks.

'Sabine, I know how hard it is in those early days in a law firm
– believe me I was a junior lawyer once – maybe not in a law firm
but I still remember the feeling of being totally out of my depth,
overwhelmed by the workload, and the pressure to perform. Please
contact me if there is anything I can do to help,' Max smiled. 'It
could be only a matter of finding out a case reference or a precedent
but if I can help, I am happy to. Sometimes just knowing there is
someone to talk something over with a person who is away from
the firm can help. Like having a safety net, I suppose. Don't forget –
anytime.' All of this was delivered with a warm and genuine smile.
Sabine couldn't help but smile in return and acknowledged that
having such a resource would be welcome.

'Like a buddy I suppose.'

'Exactly.'

The door shut on the two men and Sabine and Stella turned to
each other with a smile.

'Wow!' said Stella. 'I knew Sam was rather lovely in a scruffy big
brother sort of way, but that Max is gorgeous. If he is the Max you
met at your father's funeral service how come you haven't chased
him up until now. Just think if you hadn't met him at tonight's *do*
then we might still be waiting.'

'We?'

'Yeah. We. If you aren't interested, I might try. Although I think
I might be wasting my time. He seemed to only have eyes for you.'

With a roll of her eyes Sabine laughed, 'I haven't got time for
romance, but maybe he might be useful as a sort of mentor. I have
the funny feeling after today that I'm going to need all the help
I can get.'

Later on, as she lay upstairs in her bed, Sabine mentally ran
through the events of that day. All in all, she decided it hadn't been
too bad. Work although confusing and rather nerve wracking would
surely improve once she got the hang of it. After all she had now
completed her first advice – or her first draft. And she had new
buddies to share her stories with. Of course, there was always Stella,

her dear and oh so sensible friend for so many years but a friend at work like Amy – someone who would be sharing in the same challenges could only be a benefit. And then Max and Sam – what was there not to like?

With a sigh, she rolled over and immediately fell asleep. A short while later a small but determined dog leapt onto the bed and snuggled into the crook of the unconscious woman's legs. Just like on any other night.

# Chapter Eight

## Andre

The next day at work was exactly as Sabine had expected – frantic. Her draft advice had been returned by Rhys with suggested changes marked in the margins. All the suggested changes made sense she supposed and with a sinking heart Sabine set to rewriting her advice trying to ignore the other work that still needed to be completed.

Yet by mid-afternoon she was done and feeling rather happy with the product of her labours. All her work was now finished and further tasks yet to be allocated. Time now for a break before her bosses realised she had nothing else to do. A quick glance in the direction of their adjoining offices and she saw the doors to both Rhys' and Fran's offices were tightly closed. That meant they were busy, and she now had time to focus on something else. And there was one task in particular that Sabine knew needed doing. That was to find Andre. She could feel her fingers tingling in anticipation as she stretched her arms above her prior to starting the internet search. Sabine had always enjoyed the excitement of a quest to solve a puzzle. The more complicated the better. But today, thanks to the wonders of the internet her hunt was soon over. Andre was extremely easy to track down. Unlike her mother he had not strayed far from his original place of employment. When Andre's career as principal dancer with the Classical Ballet

45

School had ended, he had remained with the organisation in a new role as choreographer. Over the years his skill had developed, and Andre had since choreographed many successful seasons not only for that ballet school but also as guest choreographer for several overseas companies.

There was even an entry on him on Wikipedia which Sabine studied intently before trawling the various social media pages to identify a way to contact him. Soon she found a Facebook page for Andre and after studying recent photos – he was still awfully good looking in that well-groomed way that dancers never lost – she sent a message saying she was Anna's daughter and would like to make contact on the phone number she provided. The message sent; Sabine leaned back in her chair wondering how long it would be until she received a response.

The answer was – almost immediately. A message pinged on her phone:

*Lovely to hear from you. I've often wondered what happened to Anna's little girl. Last time I heard about you; you were a wild little toddler who ran everywhere. I hope you and your mother are coping alright? I read the news about your father and am so sorry for you both. Is there anything you want me to do? I would be very happy to talk to you if you want to ring me. My number is \*\*\*\*\*.*

He answered on the first ring.

'Hello?' and when Sabine introduced herself Andre's excitement screamed down the phone.

'I can't believe I'm talking to Anna's little girl. After all these years. I have to sit down. Hold on – this is all too much. I don't know where to start. How are you? How is your mother? What has been happening? Obviously, I had already heard the sad news about your father and I'm very sorry - but what else? Does your mother still dance? Is she well and …'?

Sabine couldn't help laughing as she was bombarded with this stream of questions and drawing breath, she interrupted the flow.

'Enough. We're both fine. Rather sad of course and trying to sort out life without dad in it. But I know we will be OK. It's just,' and there she paused not sure how to express herself and then in typical Sabine style she launched right in.

'You see the reason I contacted you was that it was only the other day that I discovered your connection with mum. I could see you were once so close, and I was hoping you might want to meet up with us soon. I think Mum could do with some of her old friends at the moment and I didn't know who else to ask.'

Silence at the other end of the phone. The silence dragged on for so long that Sabine started to wonder if the line had dropped out.

'Are you still there Andre?'

'Yes, yes I'm here. You've given me a bit of a shock and I was wondering how to respond. You know it has been years since I last spoke to your mother. What makes you think she might want to resume contact? Does she know you are talking to me now?'

'No, she doesn't. Look we found the letter you wrote my dad in his papers – the one where you said you would keep away. Mum had never seen it before and seemed surprised. Something about her reaction made me think that she would welcome seeing you again. She spoke of your time together very fondly.'

'We were the best.' Sabine could hear Andre's enthusiasm in his tone of voice. The excitement palpable. 'What a team we were. When we danced it was pure instinct – like we were one. We just flowed. Oh, how I missed her when she left. I had hoped Anna would return once her injuries healed and she became bored with married life. But I never heard from her and as I promised to make no contact there was nothing I could do.'

Sabine could hear a deep intake of breath before Andre continued: 'Look I don't want to intrude but if your mother would like to see me, I will be there in a shot. You've now got my phone number. Check with Anna and if she agrees we can catch up. I'm usually based in Melbourne but am in Sydney at the moment. However, what with practice and performances my time is limited … Anna will understand that. Now that's a thought. Maybe you could both come to a performance and then we could do something afterwards?'

\*\*\*

That evening Sabine rang Anna and invited herself and Grover over to dinner at her mother's house. She now thought of it as her mother's house, but it had once been her home – the family home until mid-way through university when she had moved out and set up a household with Stella.

'Sorry Ma but I do have to bring the dog. He hasn't seen me all day and besides he kinda likes you.'

'It seems to me that he has a funny way of showing it – chewing my shoes and digging up my garden. Bring him if you must but I warn you there won't be much for dinner. Just leftovers – for you and for that dog.'

'Fine by me and to be honest leftovers is more than we have in our house.'

Arriving at her once family home Sabine felt undecided. Since she now lived elsewhere did that mean she was like any other visitor and ring the doorbell or could she still let herself in unannounced? A dilemma left unresolved as her mother, alerted by the barking from a small fluffy dog, opened the door as they approached along the front path.

Judging from Grover's reaction, as soon as he saw Sabine's mother he knew she must be the most important person in the universe. Here was someone he recognised, a friend and with frenetic jumping he hurled himself at this person whom he knew just wanted to see him.

With batting hands she pushed him away whilst complaining to her daughter that she really needed to control her wild dog.

'Really Sabine. This dog is too much. Can't you control him?'

'Grover's happy to see you. In fact, more than excited – ecstatic. He adores you.'

A small smile flickered across Anna's face, as if she was quietly pleased that she invoked such adulation and with a graceful half turn she strode away towards the kitchen.

'Come on you terrible dog. I might as well spoil you seeing as you will be my only grandchild. I have some treats for you in the pantry.'

Grover's vocabulary might be limited but he knew the word *treat* when he heard it and with an excited bark he scampered after Anna leaving Sabine to shut the front door and follow the noisy pair.

Dog settled and sometime later while Sabine and her mother shared a rather basic dinner – of cheese, biscuits and some tossed salad, accompanied by a rather delicious white wine from her father's cellar– Sabine took a deep breath but before she could continue her mother interrupted.

'I hope what you are about to tell me isn't too serious. After the last few weeks, I'm not sure I can take anything more. Please don't tell me you're ill or anything like that. I've been on tenterhooks all afternoon since you rang. It's really not like you to invite yourself to dinner at short notice. I just knew it had to be something bad...'

Sabine reached forward and took both her mother's trembling hands in her much larger ones. Aware of the worried expression she could see on her mother's face she did her best to speak slowly (always a challenge) and to maintain a calm tone – even though she was not sure how her mother would receive the news.

'No Ma. All is good. Work is full on of course but I seem to be managing and they haven't sacked me yet!' She grinned. 'But there is something else I wanted to share with you. You know when we cleared out Dad's chambers the other day and I found that letter from Andre?'

'Yeees' her mother said slowly.

Trying to sound confident and chirpy Sabine continued 'Well you never guess what? I tracked him down and have spoken to Andre who would love to see you again and meet me. Actually, it wasn't that hard to find him – five minutes on the computer and I had nailed him! Anyway, Andre suggested we go to a performance and then meet afterwards. It's a bit hard to arrange to meet any other time, as he has so many commitments. It's fortunate that he is currently here in Sydney for the ballet season and Andre said he would love to see you again and meet me.'

'You spoke to him?'

'Yes of course, and he was so friendly. Don't shake your head ma. This is for the best you know. Isn't it time?'

Her mother withdrew her hands and looking down as she continued to shake her head.

'Sabine I'm not sure I can do that. Meeting Andre will just remind me of all that I gave up. My old life with Andre is over and it will be too painful to go back again. I know you mean well but really - I think you are asking too much. No, it won't work,' she said quite definitely, accompanied by more head shaking.

'Ma just think on it. Andre was once a very special friend and said he would really like to see you again. And think of me – I know nothing of your old friends, and this would be a chance to learn more about your old life. Maybe – just maybe - catching up with Andre might give you some ideas on what to do next. After all, with dad gone it must be time to think of focussing on yourself – or me if you prefer.' Sabine preened and with a flourish of her head grinned at her mother.

Her mother sighed. 'You're right as always, my very bossy daughter. It's just terrifying – what will he think of me? An ordinary housewife with grey hair.'

'Ordinary? In your dreams! And if there are any grey hairs you need superpower vision to find them. Be brave mum. I'll prop you up, don't worry. So, it's decided then? I'll contact Andre and see if he can obtain any spare tickets for later this week. We will get decked out in our very best and we will blow them out of the water! You'll see. Trust me - you won't regret it.'

'Sabine how could I think I would ever be able to resist you?'

# Chapter Nine

# A night at the ballet

Andre's delighted response was immediate when Sabine informed him they would be happy to meet him at the ballet. Tickets were arranged for that Friday night's performance. Sabine could tell Andre was excited about meeting her mother by the way he bombarded her with texts about where they should go afterwards. Excited and anxious. Clearly it was important to him for the evening to be a success and in a way she agreed. Sabine suspected Andre had only one chance to get this right and renew that friendship. However, he wasn't the only one to be anxious. Her mother was also driving her mad with her frequent texts worrying about whether this was a good idea and then about what to wear and how long would they have to stay.

In the end it was all too much. *'Enough!'* She texted to Andre. *'Let's just go to wherever you usually go to after a performance. That will be fine. Even drinks in the foyer will be fine. Don't fuss!'*

*'Enough'* she texted to her mother. *'It will be fine. You might even enjoy it. At the very least we will enjoy a beautiful ballet and maybe have a glass (or two) of sparkling. Get your hair done and wear one of those gorgeous designer outfits that clutter your wardrobe. I will collect you from home at about 6 so I can be sure you won't chicken out. Now I have to work so I do get to have Friday evening off. Don't forget 6pm — dressed and ready to go xxxxx'*

Her tough love must have worked as both Andre and Anna left her alone for the next two days. Which was just as well, as her workload seemed to increase daily. Requests to draft advice on issues she knew nothing about. Legal research rushed and hopefully accurate and feelings of being overwhelmed by the sheer volume of the demands on her time by various members of the firm.

Fran must have noticed as one afternoon she called Sabine into her office to, as she put it *review* her first few weeks with the firm.

They settled into two red leather tub chairs facing each other across a glass coffee table in the corner of Fran's office. Fran busied herself pouring them both a glass of water from the stylish jug that her secretary kept topped up during the day and passed one glass to Sabine.

'So, how's it going Sabine? Is it all starting to make sense?'

Sabine wasn't sure how to respond to that. Nothing made sense and most days she felt like she was mired in mud or crawling through custard. Custard was a more attractive analogy, loving food as she did, but either way, she often felt stuck, Yet she was enough of her father's daughter to know that it was important to never show weakness.

'You know. It's all so new. A big change from uni, but I feel like I'm making progress. So much to do and so much variety in the work. I just hope I'm meeting expectations. How do you think I'm going?' (That's what her father would recommend. Answer a question with a question.)

It seemed to work. Fran was immediately distracted.

'You're right. Legal practice is such a big step up from university. And the variety is something that can be challenging. Learning to manage multiple tasks sometimes takes a bit of getting used to. And so important to be organised. But I hear from my colleagues that you are progressing and from what I have seen I think you are making a good start. So well done Sabine.'

And with that she was dismissed. As Fran got up to answer her phone she smiled at Sabine and said how pleased they had time to have *this little chat*. Sabine wandered out of the office back to her cubicle wondering what had really happened. Was being told she was *progressing* a good or bad thing? Would it always be this chaotic?

'How did it go?' whispered Amy from the adjoining cubicle.

'I have no idea. I'm *progressing* but as to whether that is forwards or backwards is unclear. But at least Fran is still smiling at me and they're giving me work to do – so much work to do – so I suppose it is all OK. What about you? Have you had your review yet?'

'Yesterday. Apparently, I think they consider my progress to be acceptable – possibly. Although I was given a list of things to improve on – more attention to detail etc. That would be so easy if I knew exactly what I was meant to be doing. But I suppose it will all become clear in the end' she said with a slightly watery smile.

'Yes, it will become clear when we are sacked' said Sabine gloomily. Not one to be gloomy for long she brightened as a new thought entered her head. 'Enough of that. I refuse to be despondent when I have tickets to tonight's performance at the ballet. In fact, I'm about to sneak off to the toilets to get changed and then go collect my mother. An early mark for me for a change. Will you cover for me if someone comes around? I'll make sure I leave my jacket on my chair, so it looks like I am still at work. Is that alright with you?'

A wave and a nod were all that she received in response. It was clear Amy was frantically working to a deadline.

Sabine knew that the events of that evening would be a big thing. She couldn't help but hope that meeting Andre was going to be the right thing to help propel her mother out of the current pit of grief. But there was every risk her mother would back out of her agreed commitment to go. She was well aware how reluctant Anna had been to consent to this outing. With that thought in mind Sabine reached for her phone and dialled. Anna answered on the first ring.

'Ma it's me.'

'Of course, it's you. I can see your number on the call display. What is the problem?' Sabine noted this was said in a slightly hopeful tone.

'I'm just checking you are OK for tonight. I'll drop by at around 6 to collect you – remember?'

'Sabine dear. There's no need to fuss. And you do not need to collect me from home like I'm some geriatric old dear. I'm perfectly capable of meeting you there. How about we meet in the foyer at about 6.30 and we can share a drink and some polite chit chat. I will be there on time, which knowing you is more than you will be.'

'Promise?'

'Of course.'

And she was. By the time Sabine arrived – yes, after the agreed time – this was Sabine after all - her mother was serenely sitting in a tub chair in the Opera House foyer, the crowd swirling around her.

'Sorry I'm late, but not by much. Give us a hug. My don't you look nice.'

Anna rose and gently reached up to clasp her towering daughter and then stepped back to consider her.

'You look pretty good yourself. It's almost time to go inside. Why don't we leave those drinks until later – maybe at interval?'

'Yep. It can keep till half time! Come on then.'

Arm in arm they headed for the designated doorway ready to show the usher the tickets clutched tightly in Sabine's hand. Two women dressed in black - of course - and each handsome in their own way. One small boned and dainty with hair perfectly and smoothly styled into a French roll, her long sleeved cross over jersey dress swirling with every gliding step taken. The other so much taller, clad in a sheer sparkling top, her narrow legged black pants and stiletto shoes emphasising the legs that seemed to go forever. Her shiny long blonde hair bouncing with every energetic step.

Now Sabine had never been one for ballet. Ballet lessons had been discontinued early on in her childhood when it became clear she neither had the build, nor the interest in persevering with this discipline. More active pursuits were for her and she quickly turned to surfing and basketball. As a result, there was very little she knew about what she was about to watch. Apart from the title that is - *Swan Lake*. Well, the title gave it away. Clearly it was something about a swan and she vaguely knew involved something about a *good* swan and a *bad* swan. She'd seen the blockbuster Hollywood movie years ago about the ballerina rehearsing for the performance and slowly going mad. That much she knew and she supposed the story would be easy to follow. But in the end the performance, delightful though it was, did not grip her attention half as much as the performance quietly unfolding in the seat next to her.

Shortly after the overture was completed and the performance commenced Sabine became aware of her mother leaning forward, hands tightly clasped as she gazed intently at the dancers on the stage below. She soon noticed how Anna gently tapped one hand against the other and swayed in time to the music. From time to time she nodded at what Sabine thought must be in approval at some particularly special movement by a dancer.

At interval, Anna was aglow and full of conversation.

'This is tremendous. I had forgotten how much I love *Swan Lake*. It was always a delight to dance in this ballet. Such a classic and how kind of Andre to invite us.'

'And how kind of Andre to organise drinks and chocolates for us at half time' said Sabine sipping from a fluted champagne glass. 'I could get used to this.'

The second half proceeded smoothly. The story line predictable in its way, although Sabine privately thought the prince must be a fool to be deluded by the black swan. With the music swirling around them the performance came to its dramatic conclusion as the Prince and Odette the white swan drowned in what Sabine thought must be meant to be a lake and by their death breaking the wicked spell. So, a happy ending of sorts, but not in her opinion a satisfactory one. Still her mother seemed quite content as she leant back in her seat and with a happy sigh and a smile she spoke:

'That was lovely, and a pretty good performance by the principal dancers,' Anna beamed. 'Although, I think the girls in the chorus need to work a bit more on coordinating their dancing. They are meant to be in time after all. But I suppose Andre noticed that.'

'Noticed what?' A voice came from behind them as Anna leapt up and in one smooth movement turned and hugged a man whom Sabine assumed was Andre.

Once a dancer always a dancer Sabine thought as she gazed at the two of them now exchanging excited greetings. Andre was not a lot taller than her mother's. Probably five foot eight in the old language and so slim, with dark hair like her mother and holding himself beautifully just like her mother and any other ex-dancer she assumed. Their colouring and features so similar they could almost be siblings. In mid-sentence Anna turned and gestured towards Sabine.

'But I forget myself. Allow me to introduce my daughter, Sabine whom I have to thank for making contact with you. I suspect if not for her we would not be here tonight. I owe her a debt of gratitude.'

Andre moved forward and reaching up he kissed Sabine on both cheeks.

'So lovely to meet you at last. My, my, we won't be making a dancer out of you', he said as he stepped back and took in Sabine's height. 'There's not much of your mother in you – maybe you have her beautiful personality? Yes, I can see you do', he added and then continued 'But enough of the chit chat. I want to introduce you both to the company. Anna they're so excited to be finally meeting you. You have been such a mystery to the young ones. The way you disappeared from public view at the height of your fame. They almost can't believe you are real. Now come this way. Oh, and don't you just love these seats I organised for you?'

With their profuse thanks ringing in the air the two women found themselves shushed by Andre, then herded downstairs towards the stage, and directed through the wings out towards the back.

Sabine tried not to gawk as she followed the other two through the cavernous backstage. Never having been behind the scenes before, she had not realised it could be so large – almost like another theatre with corridors that branched out in various directions. She realised that it would be very easy for her to get lost in such a maze and quickly caught up with her mother and Andre who were striding ahead as if they were both familiar with the layout of the place. Snippets of the conversation drifting back to her confirmed this.

'And remember how we danced this very same ballet here all those years ago?' she heard her mother exclaim.

'Oh, I do Anna dear. We were fantastic. Need I say we shone. If those young ones from tonight's performance could have seen us perform, they would realise how off the mark they are. I can see we are going to have to do a lot of work on them tomorrow.' And then as if struck by a sudden thought he continued: 'Now there's a thought. I say Anna. I don't suppose you can spare time to sit in on our rehearsal tomorrow morning. Your insight would be most helpful. I'm sure having seen tonight's performance you might have a few suggestions?'

Perfect, thought Sabine. Just what was needed for her mother. A new or should that be - a rekindled interest for her mother. Something to distract her from grief.

Clearly her mother thought so too. Her response immediate and as enthusiastic as Sabine's unspoken thoughts.

'Andre I would be delighted to sit in tomorrow. Nothing would give me greater pleasure. It will be just like old times us working together. Although this time I won't have the aches and pains or do all the hard-physical work.' In a more muted tone so quiet that Sabine found herself hurrying in order to overhear she continued. 'Mind you I think the swan maidens could do with a bit more work. Is there an injury there? One swan seemed a bit hesitant. The principals' performance was impressive. But, as you and I know, there is always room for improvement,' said with a little laugh to which Andre responded with a chuckle.

The remainder of the evening passed in a blur of colour, movement and delighted conversations. Sabine found herself leaning against the side wall as she watched her mother, the centre of attention surrounded by an admiring crowd. She felt no need to become part of the event. Her mother she thought had never looked so alive, visibly glowing with delight as the dancers and all the others in the company made it clear how much they admired her. Anna laughed as she and Andre shared their tales of their successes and failures to the amusement of the company. With linked arms Anna and Andre sparked off each other, as with each tale their shared exploits became more and more exaggerated.

Sabine realised it had been a long time since she had seen her mother so energised and happy. The mother she knew was calm, organised – serene. Or was it really that she was depressed? Not one for deep thoughts Sabine shook her head and decided that such analysis was unnecessary when clearly tonight was a hit. She was quietly congratulating herself for such inspired organisation when a voice intruded:

'Penny for them. Or should I say a cent for your thoughts. Although I suspect that kinda devalues them.'

She turned and there was Andre who somehow had snuck away from the adoring throng.

'I was just thinking how happy my mother looks. Like she is back now in her home environment where she really belongs. There was so much I didn't know about her ballet career, and I still find it hard to understand how she was able to walk away from all this camaraderie and give up her passion for dance just like that. Seeing how happy she is tonight I'm hoping there must be some way we can help her regain her sparkle.'

'Don't worry little one,' laughed Andre 'Probably not the accurate description for you. But to me you will always be Anna's *little one.*' He placed his finger on the side of his nose in the time-honoured signal for keeping a secret and continued, 'I have a plan, which has just now come to me. Little by little I intend to draw Anna back into the world she once loved. Little steps - starting tomorrow. Maybe, just maybe we can bring this frozen princess back to life.'

Secretly Sabine bristled – *frozen princess?* That was a bit much. Her mother had had a good life up to now. OK so she had not been Miss Vivacity in her dual role as the Judge's wife and Sabine's mother, but she had never so much as hinted her life was less than satisfactory. Yet watching Anna engage with what Sabine could now see clearly were her type of people, her mother's tribe so to speak, she could see that this was where her mother belonged. Maybe Andre had a funny way of expressing it, but he was probably right.

But it was now time to leave. A quick glance at her watch confirmed the lateness of the hour. Making excuses to Andre she dragged her mother away from her adoring acolytes, but not before Andre promised that they would see more of Anna at rehearsal.

'Bright and early remember,' he spoke to the assembled dancers. 'And I mean bright!'

They shared a taxi to their respective homes, the journey initially silent, with mother and daughter sitting quietly, together on the back seat yet each alone in their separate thoughts. Sabine could see by a surreptitious glance at her mother that her thoughts were happy ones as was obvious by the contented smile and the way she reached out for her daughter's hand.

'Thank you, my darling daughter. And I really mean it. If it were not for you pushing me into it, I would never have found the courage to go to tonight's performance. Meeting Andre and being in that environment was way too terrifying for me to contemplate. But it was wonderful. As soon as I entered the Opera House those memories all came rushing back. The emotion and the feelings. Like a part of me that was lost had now been recovered and I once again felt whole.'

She must have sensed Sabine's reaction to these words as, still holding her daughter's hand, she gave it a gentle squeeze.

'Don't get me wrong my dear. I love you - being your mother has been one of my greatest achievements - and of course I loved your father', said almost as an afterthought. 'I hadn't before realised how much of myself I sacrificed when I married your father. My choice of course. But now,' a happy smile swept across her face.

'Now I have the opportunity to be part of that world again. Not as a dancer of course, but there must be role for me somewhere. I'm definitely going to talk to Andre about this tomorrow.'

Sabine's home was the first stop. With kisses and promises to catch up soon, she left the cab, then stood by the curb with one hand waving as she watched the taillights of the cab speed off in the direction of Vaucluse, where the once family home stood – silent and echoing – no longer a welcoming place – if it ever was. Her hand slowly fell as she turned and pushing the squeaky iron gate open. Sabine moved slowly along the path towards the front door of the compact terrace house still pondering the night's events. Stella had thoughtfully left the hall light on and there waiting for her once she opened the door was the perfect reception committee. A small fluffy dog leaping about in excitement at the return of his beloved human and coming down the hall her favourite housemate dressed in hot pink flannelette pyjamas and wearing fluffy slippers

'Why are you still up? Isn't it a workday tomorrow?'

'I wish I could have had an early night. I dream of those, but I have a case starting tomorrow and a client conference first thing in the morning. A challenge to an eviction and I was just finalising my preparation.'

Stella as a junior lawyer working for the Legal Aid Office often spent the evenings working. The office was so under resourced that even the most junior lawyers struggled under overwhelming caseloads. No wonder the staff turnover was so high even though the work done was vital. Sabine often felt concerned about the toll it was taking on Stella. The contrast between the resources available to her at *Smithtons* and what Stella had to contend with each day was stark. There seemed so much about this that was unfair, but she was already coming to learn that fairness didn't always feature in the law. The stories that Stella sometime shared with her about the life challenges faced by many of her clients made her question much that she had learned during her sheltered and privileged upbringing.

Early on she had asked Stella how she could manage to stay so positive when, day after day she heard so many harrowing tales that she knew had little hope of bringing about a positive outcome.

'It's what I have always wanted to do. To help those that often can't help themselves. To give them a chance to turn their life around. Maybe it's because of my grandparents being refugees from Italy all those years ago after the war that makes me want to do this job. I was born here of course which meant I had no first-hand experience of their journey to get to Australia. But, growing up I heard many of their harrowing tales and I remember how hard it was, not only for my grandparents, but also for my parents when I was young. We had very little, yet people were kind and helped us and my grandparents and parents worked so hard. They were all incredibly grateful to be here and so determined to create a future for my brother and I, that I feel giving back in this way is my way of saying thank you. Mind you on a bad day there are a number of my clients who aren't at all grateful for my assistance,' she laughed. 'But the small number of ones that are, the ones I have truly helped make it all worthwhile.'

Tonight, though Stella was more interested in receiving a debrief on the evening's outing.

'So out with it Beanie. Tell me. How did it go? Did your mother turn up? What was Andre like? Is he still as gorgeous as he was in those old photos? He looks about my height. Maybe I should meet him?'

'Enough with the questions. Make me a cup of tea woman and I will tell you all. Not that there is a lot to tell and forget Andre. He is way too old for you and anyway my guess is he is interested in another type of partner.'

A pot of tea made and poured the two young women sat around the small table in the kitchen, one cuddling a snuggling hound while the other, with elbows resting on table, listened in rapt attention to Sabine's account of the evening. She left nothing out: her concern that her mother would cancel, her relief that she didn't and how gorgeous Anna looked.

'No wonder people say we could be sisters rather than mother and daughter. She's barely aged at all and tonight she was so excited I swear it took 20 years off her age.'

'So, it was a success then?'

'Absolutely. Beyond my wildest dreams. Although I am hoping that I haven't set her up for a tremendous disappointment.'

Why?'

Sabine outlined Andre's plan to somehow find a role for her in the ballet company although he was vague about what and how her mother spoke in the cab about finding a part of herself again. Yet, as her dancing days were long past that would not be possible so what else could she do?'

'Well, you know what they say. Those that can't do, teach. Maybe that's a path for your mother. If nothing else maybe tonight has reawakened your mother's interest in dance. Maybe your work is done, and it is now up to Anna to find a future for herself? I know you like to organise all things and all people but perhaps just this once now that you have pointed your mother in this direction it's time for you to step back and see how things evolve?'

Later on, while lying in bed with a small dog snuggled beside her, Sabine replayed Stella's words in her head. Stella as always spoke sense. Sensible Stella as she often called her had been on point this time. Time to let go, and let her mother work it out for herself. Almost as if I'm the mother in this situation she thought. If nothing else this new interest would be a welcome distraction from grief. Yet there was a small voice whispering its discontent. Wouldn't it be nice if just once her mother turned to her for comfort? The small child that had craved a mother's affection was still there, watching and hoping that one day she would be the centre of someone's universe. But as she mentally chided herself - if it hadn't happened with her mother by now then it was most unlikely to happen.

*Get real Sabine*, she whispered to herself. *You are a big girl now. Suck it up and get on with life. Just accept that the only unconditional love you will ever receive is from your little canine friend here.* Somehow that thought made her smile and relax sufficiently for a dreamless sleep to overtake her.

# Chapter Ten

# The life of a young lawyer

Sabine stared at the typed draft advice which had been returned to her- now for the second time. Returned with a terse comment that it needed more work. A number of red scrawls decorated the work and numerous red question marks indicated that Rhys was less than satisfied with the quality of her writing on what was meant to be a straightforward piece of work.

'Why does it have to be so hard? And why can't I get what I am supposed to have left out? It's like doing a cryptic crossword deciphering his comments', Sabine said out loud groaning in frustration.'

'Here. Let me see,' came a voice from the adjoining cubicle. Amy's head popped up and was now visible just like one of those cute meercats that were so beloved by advertising gurus. 'I need a break from my project, so I'm happy to read it for you.

'Would you? You're a life saver. I have done and redone this advice so many times that it all seems like one big blur and I can no longer think straight.'

'Leave it with me. I'll read it while you go and get me a coffee and then maybe we can talk it over.'

A short while later when she returned from the downstairs café with coffees for both of them, she found Amy waiting by her desk with draft advice in hand.

'Thanks for the coffee. I really needed that. You know I think this advice you've drafted is pretty good. But as they are always telling us. *Pretty Good* is not enough for *Smithtons*,' said with a rolling of her eyes and the hint of a smile. 'And some of his comments are a bit cryptic, See this one here – *why* he writes. I'm not sure if he wants you to expand on that sentence with a bit of justification or perhaps Rhys doesn't believe you. Maybe the former? This bit here where he has written *too long*, I guess is self-explanatory. He wants you to simplify it to be a bit less legalistic. But as for all these red question marks, I just don't know. Maybe you have to get a moment of his time – that's a hard one I know - to discuss it with him?'

'I feel like such a goose. This will be my third go. But I guess you are right. I'll do another redraft then book some time with him and maybe I will never see this stupid advice again. No one told me that my exciting legal career would entail labouring over tedious drafts and redrafts. Surely there's more to it than this?'

Amy took this as a rhetorical question and with a wave and coffee in hand she scooted back to her desk.

A short while later Sabine leaned back in her chair and considered her redrafted advice. Maybe Rhys had been correct. It had been too wordy. Now pruned with surgical skill she was starting to feel like her work was starting to look polished and to the point. Except she had yet to address the issues raised by all those red question marks. Watching Fran approach, she wondered if she could seek her assistance. Maybe not, as she took note of the handbag and briefcase in Fran's hands.

'I have to get home. A bit of emergency with the nanny and of course I can't get hold of my husband. Why are men never around when you need them? Anyway, it would appear that you are managing perfectly fine on your own and don't need me. It looks like you will be here awhile, so I've forwarded my phone to you in case there are any calls. See you tomorrow.'

Clearly, she was now on her own. If only there was someone that she could talk this advice through with and try to determine what was missing. Someone a bit senior to whom it didn't matter if she was to reveal her complete ignorance, which was how she currently felt. And then it dawned on Sabine that all along there was the perfect sounding board and he had already said he was happy to help. Now where was his card? She scrabbled in her handbag and eventually located said card lurking at the bottom entangled in the everyday detritus that was the reality of most handbags. Picking off a congealed mint she peered at the barely distinguishable details and just as she was reaching for the phone it rang. Could he be ringing her? Or was it Stella wondering where she was. It was after 7pm after all.

No. It was someone else. A male voice and an angry one at that boomed down the phone before Sabine could even get a word out.

'Where are you? I've just got home to find the house in an uproar. The nanny's not here. The neighbour's holding the baby and you know how I feel about strangers holding our baby. Get your arse home now or there will be trouble. You useless woman.'

The voice was still ranting as Sabine gently hung up terminating the call. Somehow, she knew it would be unwise to even speak to the caller who she assumed could only be Fran's husband. The call must have come through on Fran's line which had been switched through to her. It was probably better that she didn't speak. For a moment she sat still contemplating the significance of what she had just heard. Poor Fran. The Fran she knew at work – calm, competent and friendly must be living in two worlds – and by the sounds, the world she confronted at home was in marked contrast to what she experienced every day at work. And a small baby being raised in such an environment? That poor child. Sabine was at a loss as to whether she should or could say anything to Fran when next she saw her. How could she speak of such personal concerns when she barely knew her boss and when Fran was a senior member of the firm. It was a boundary she was reluctant to cross – but yet – there was a young person involved. Maybe Stella might have some suggestions. Yes, Stella, the oh so wise would know what to do.

The business card still in her hand she looked down and with a mental shake refocussed on the task at hand. Max answered the phone at the first ring. His hello was hesitant as if he didn't know the identity of the caller. After all – why should he? She had never rung before.

'Max it's Sabine Faulkner. Remember me? I hope you don't mind me calling but you said last time we spoke I could call if I needed help.'

A brief hesitation, almost as if he was trying to recall who this person was on the other end of the phone.

'No problem and of course I remember you. By the way I really enjoyed our chat at that drinks event and thank you again for dinner at your place.'

'It was nothing - just take away and you guys organised it while I walked the dog.'

A pause and then they both started to talk at once. Polite laughter as Max insisted Sabine speak first.

'You see I'm stuck on a legal advice I've been working on for what seems like ages. I know my supervising partner is not happy with it as he has returned it twice. He seems to disagree with my legal analysis of the relevant case law – or I think that is what he means by all the red question marks he has in the margins. But I'm stuck. I've done my research and I can't see what I am missing. You said you were happy to be a sounding board for me. Is that still on offer?'

'Of course.' Sabine could tell by the tone of his voice that there was a hint of amusement and tried not to feel resentful. Sabine knew she was not an idiot, but she really was stuck. When Max asked her to summarise the issue and then read out her legal analysis, she swallowed her resentment and did so.

'I see. You know I think that reads pretty clearly but could benefit from being a bit more direct and less verbose. And the case law seems on point. But I'm wondering if there is another case – a recent one that might also apply. Give me a moment and I will do a bit of searching. Maybe I can find the citation.' She could hear the keyboard clicking as Max searched for the details of the case he mentioned.

'Ah here it is. Only decided six months ago but it might be relevant. I'll text you the name and citation. Look it up and see if the facts in that matter are on point. Perhaps that is what he is after?'

'Maybe. Thanks a heap. You really are a life saver. I'll get onto it right away and maybe I will be able to get rid of this advice tonight. I never want to see it again!'

A snort of laughter.

'It rarely works that way. With your luck this will probably be the start of a close and personal working relationship with this client!'

'No way. I'm the junior lawyer, remember. Always in the wings.'

'It seems to me that this junior lawyer has worked long enough today. Fancy a drink?'

Sabine considered the amount of work left to do and shook her head. Then realising this wasn't a conference call she spoke.

'Sadly. Not today. I'd really like to, but I must finish this advice and then get home. Hopefully it won't take much longer. Maybe tomorrow? Early breakfast?'

With the plans made they ended the call, and Sabine with fresh energy returned to her work. The office lay silent and deserted. All the other lawyers and the support staff were long gone. The only noise was the gentle hum from her computer and in the distance the muted sound of a vacuum cleaner at work.

***

There was no need to set the alarm for the next morning. At the very hint of first light Sabine bounced out of bed, fully awake and fizzing with excitement. For reasons she couldn't yet discern the thought of meeting Max again was most welcome. But first there was the matter of taking a small dog for a quick walk around the neighbourhood, and a forbidden run in the park. This early in the morning there would be no one there to object to an energetic fluffy dog scampering around off the lead, except for the homeless people who would have spent the night sheltering on the benches or in the bushes. But as Sabine and her doggy friend were well known to them, she knew there would be no comment, other than a muttered response of thanks when she distributed the freshly made finger buns from the local baker. Although she always made sure she kept one back to share with Grover.

Home, dog fed and after a quick shower and once changed into an outfit suitable for a junior lawyer (black trouser suit with lacy camisole), Sabine set off on her bicycle heading into the city for her breakfast assignation.

For once she was early. Something she was sure her mother would not believe. If only she was here to see her ever so punctual daughter. But then again, possibly not. She found a table near the window of the bustling café. Even at 7.30 in the morning, the place was almost full. The café almost completely populated by people just like her, men and women uniformly dressed in black, navy or dark grey pinstripe. Glancing around at her companions she made a mental note to break out a bit of colour in her everyday work attire. Nothing too dramatic. A light grey perhaps?

Sabine saw Max approach and had the opportunity to examine him before he squeezed past the queue waiting by the take-away window. He really was rather gorgeous. Tall, dark and handsome, as those stories often said. Dark hair cut stylishly short, a strong jawline and straight nose. She could see his dark eyes glancing around looking for her as he entered the café and then his welcoming smile and a wave as he caught sight of Sabine.

So it wasn't just her that was pleased to be here this morning.

Greetings exchanged. No kisses – yet. But there was genuine warmth of the greeting which was apparent in Max's crinkling eyes as he smiled and the happy tone of his voice.

'Good morning. I hope you are feeling much more positive than you were sounding last night. You sounded quite down. I was worried about you.' His hand reached across the table and briefly touched her hand. She felt the warmth and tingle from his touch move up her hand. A reaction from her body to this man, something she had never felt before with any other person. A sense of loss as his hand was withdrawn and a wish that she could prolong their contact.

The menu perused and orders taken they settled down into conversation. Given Sabine knew very little about this man she found it surprisingly easy to chat with him. Max seemed genuinely interested in her feelings and background. She found herself sharing her concerns about her mother's wellbeing, something she had been reluctant to fully divulge to anyone else, even Stella. Max's warm brown eyes registered concern about what she was saying and then with expert skill steered the discussion onto Sabine's wellbeing. He was a barrister after all and knew how to manipulate the conversation.

Sabine opened up on the weirdness of a family life absent a father. Especially someone like the Judge who had a view on everything and a determination that this life should run exactly as he directed.

'You know I hadn't realised how controlling he was until he was dead. Although it was a subtle form of control. Not overt and certainly I never felt like he was a dictator. I just appreciated how much more pleasant our family life was when I basked in the glow of his approval. I suspect my mother felt the same. I sense she is still sad but there is something else. These days she seems much more relaxed and dare I say it, possibly feeling a bit optimistic now she has the chance to start a new life focussing on her passions rather than his.'

With the arrival of breakfast, scrambled eggs and bacon for Max and Eggs Benedict for Sabine, conversation turned to *that* advice and Sabine's revision.

'Thank you for your help by the way. I really was stuck and your feedback helped me see the issue in a new light. I stayed back for another hour or so after we spoke and finished the draft. I've incorporated that case you referred me to and now it's with Rhys for review and hopefully approval. I never want to see it again!' Sabine shook her head and grimaced, not because the food she was shovelling into her mouth was bad, but because of the thought of having to revisit that work.

'You know I am beginning to wonder if being a lawyer will always be this frustrating. I accept that I'm a baby lawyer and have a lot to learn but I had thought it would be more exciting than this. Stuck at my desk most of the day, sitting in on conference calls and being silent while the bosses speak – is that what my 5 years at university prepared me for?'

Sabine smiled to indicate she wasn't serious, but now the words were out in the open what she was saying felt quite accurate. Perhaps this wasn't the life for her? The life her father had mapped out for her was starting to feel strangely unappealing.

'It's hard I know.'

And there was his hand reaching across the table again. An awfully touchy man, but somehow, she didn't mind.

'Give it some time. This is your first experience with the firm and your first rotation. Maybe you haven't found the subject matter that's right for you – or the right firm for that matter. We all feel hesitant when we hit *the real world*. Believe in yourself. I do. You've spent five years reshaping your brain to think like a lawyer. Now you have to learn to apply those skills. Try to be patient. It's kind of like an apprenticeship you are on now.'

'No one told me I would still be this ignorant. I thought that once I finished my law degree I would come out of university fully fledged and able to fly. But now I'm discovering that it's not that simple. I feel like there's an abyss of total ignorance that I face every day. And to make it worse just because I'm the *Judge's daughter*, this said using her hands to indicate a quote, 'and referred to as such at *Smithtons*, there is that expectation that I have all the answers.'

Max was quietly comforting. 'You do have the answers. You've done the training and it's now a matter of learning how to apply it. Trust yourself and your instincts. Forget what other people think and remember I am here. I will always have your back.'

For some reason Sabine found those words reassuring and smiled her appreciation.

Breakfast and conversation over, they spoke their quick farewells outside the café. Max had a pre-hearing conference and then a trial to attend and Sabine, well Sabine had no idea of what awaited her. But after Max's stirring words she felt sufficiently confident to take on whatever was dished out to her. After all, hadn't her nickname at school been Val, and like any Valkyrie woman she should be up for anything.

As she wheeled her bike and walked the few blocks to the office, Sabine reviewed her breakfast with Max. There was something about him she liked. He seemed kind and caring. Genuine. His touch made her tingle and the brief kiss on the cheek and a gentle hug as they departed made her want to prolong the encounter. Maybe next time? And she was sure there would be a next time. He made that clear before they went their separate ways. There was so much more she wanted to know about this highly attractive man. Reviewing their conversation Sabine realised he had been reticent about his own background. She sensed some sadness might be lurking in Max's past. Not that he seemed unhappy with his present life. But she sensed there was a back story there that needed exploring. And she was just the person to do it.

# Chapter Eleven

# All about Max

Max Sumner was an enigma. Something he occasionally acknowledged to himself on one of those rare reflective moments. Handsome, articulate, educated and of course well-dressed, he was popular with everyone, yet self-contained and kept himself slightly aloof and at a distance from others. Slightly mysterious. Even those so-called friends, when pressed admitted they were only familiar with his present and not his past.

Christened David James Sumner he was born and raised in the outer western suburbs of Sydney. Raised by Christine, a single mother, who struggled to feed and clothe her son and daughter by working two jobs – shift work at a local clothing factory and at weekends at a nearby café. Max's older sister Leanne, a resentful babysitter for her little brother was not much of a mother substitute. With an often-absent mother and a disdainful sister Max quickly learned that the only person he could rely upon was himself.

There was no father in young Max's life. He was long gone.

'And good riddance to him too,' spat out Christine when questioned by concerned neighbours and friends.

Max grew up a solitary child – content with his own company and complicated imaginary games. He would have remained that way – a slight reserved child – a loner – except for the vigilance of the sports master at the local high school. Observing Max's ball skills during the class sports lesson that teacher identified his potential. And before he knew it Max's life expanded. In summer it was cricket, in winter it was soccer as football was called in those days. With sporting prowess came friendship with other boys, attention from the girls and a way to distance himself from his homelife. By now Max's sister had left school and at 18 was working *in retail* as she called it – serving at the counter of the local hardware store. Never home - either at work or out with the various tradies that she met and served during working hours or in their panel vans. Served so well that it wasn't long before she was pregnant and wed to Wayne and moved several suburbs away.

His mother, who you would expect to have reduced her working hours as the demands on her purse lessened, still kept up her two jobs – almost as a way of filling time. Their house, a government provided home on a public housing estate, looked more and more unloved with each passing year. Paint peeling off the walls, the garden and lawn dead, it looked even worse than its neglected neighbours.

When Max turned 18, he made a number of life-changing decisions. The results from his final year exams were outstanding – of course – and ensured acceptance into an economics/law degree at Sydney University the oldest and most *establishment* university in the land. He immediately knew that this was not the place for *David Sumner*, the poor kid from the outskirts of Sydney. If he was to succeed and be someone people would be drawn to, he needed to project an image – become someone else. As he had read: success breeds success. And he *so* wanted a life that was bigger and brighter than what he had experienced so far.

Thus, David James Sumner became Max Hugo Sumner, a name that hinted at an upper-class past – or so he hoped. Changing his name by deed poll was simple. Explaining why to his mother was not so simple, but then, as he justified it to himself, she was rapidly retreating into his past and as far as he could see there would be no role for her in his glorious future. As for his sister – she was long gone as far as he was concerned.

During his university years Max set about creating the future he desired for himself. With his absolute focus academic success was assured, and with it came the scholarships that eased his financial burden. Max's good looks and sporting prowess opened many doors – holidays at Palm Beach in sumptuous mansions, sailing on the harbour and numerous invitations to Eastern Suburbs villas owned by the parents of his fellow students. Max was a quick learner. With each new experience Max observed and absorbed the behaviour of those around him: how to speak, which cutlery or wine glass to use and how to entertain his hosts with engaging conversation. His place in this gilded environment was soon taken for granted by all.

Many years later, his studies completed Max was the proud recipient of a combined Economics/Law degree. By now he was a man in his mid- 20's who had transformed into an urbane and sophisticated man – charming to all and relaxed in any surroundings. It helped that he was very easy on the eye – maturing into a tall man with an impressive physique kept toned by all those sporting activities. There were many that admired him – male and female, but none were allowed to get too close. Keeping people at a distance and thus preserving the secret of his past had become almost automatic. That slight hint of reserve in his behaviour enhanced his mysterious charm and made him even more popular.

Securing the Associate position with Judge Antony Faulkner was an unexpected achievement. The competition for the job was way beyond anything he had ever before experienced. It was with a mixture of relief and anxiety he accepted the offer. At the same time he wondered whether this would be the moment when his façade of competence and assurance would be revealed for what it was -a façade – and that underneath still lurked a shy, insecure little boy afraid of failure.

Judge Faulkner turned out to be yet another outstanding influence in Max's life. Tall and austere, with a patrician bearing, a fine head of hair and an impressive nose, Judge Faulkner brooked no fools and would be ruthless in demolishing with a few well-placed words anyone whose incompetence or idiocy interfered with his own agenda. On the other hand, if he saw merit in someone the Judge would go out of his way to develop it. There must have been something he observed in Max that warranted nurturing. Over the year Max spent working as an Associate the Judge kept his temper and caustic wit under control – at least when directed at Max with the result that Max had a masterclass in the practical side of court appearances. He had always intended to go to the Bar and practice as a barrister once his time as a Judge's Associate came to an end. Early on he had shared this ambition with the Judge. Maybe it was because of this disclosure but throughout their twelve months together the Judge was diligent in bringing to Max's attention details of the failings of those who appeared before him.

'Put your time with me to good use Max. Make sure you learn from other people's mistakes Max and be better than these idiots that appear before me.'

And he did.

Max was unsure how he really felt about the Judge. In some ways they had much in common – their reserved manner and the sense of not giving too much away. Yet there was also much to respect – the Judge's work ethic, his intellect and constant questioning of the evidence. The way the Judge drew a line between work and home life. was also something Max admired. There were no shared disclosures about family, which Max appreciated. He was relieved to find that the Judge had no interest in Max's background, or his life spent outside working hours. All the Judge cared about was how Max would assist him with the Judge's work and that suited Max just fine.

It then came as a surprise at the end of one busy week, that the Judge asked Max if he wanted to join him for a drink to celebrate a successful six months in the job. How could he refuse? At least Max was reassured that the Judge would take control of any conversation as he always did. He expected any discussion would be about legal cases and work. But it wasn't. With a sinking feeling he realised the Judge was out to grill Max – about Max.

'Tell me about yourself. I've seen for myself that you have the makings of an excellent lawyer, but what else? What is your background?'

'Nothing of any note sir,' said Max trying to shut down this line of conversation.

But the Judge was not to be deterred. He was skilled in asking the difficult questions.

'Parents? Siblings?'

'My mother brought my sister and me up. My sister is older than me and is now married and recently has had a baby.' Max hoped that this was enough information to satisfy the Judge, but as a further diversion he continued, – 'and of course I have always loved sport. You know First Eleven in cricket at Uni and occasional rugby. (Soccer had long been passed over for the socially acceptable Rugby Union - the game played by those who had attended the *best schools* and ensured his admission into their select social network.)

A successful distraction as with that the Judge launched into a discourse concerning his own sporting successes over the years.

Further discussion ensued about the merits of various sports and then it was time to leave. Thanking the Judge Max stood to go, feeling relieved at having got off so lightly.

'Of course, some time you must join our little family for dinner. My daughter Sabine is studying law – still a few years to go. She's a bright young thing and I'm sure you'll have a lot in common,'

The Judge – matchmaking? Surely not! But with a glance at the Judge and his earnest expression Max was not so sure. The last thing he needed was someone who could discover his secrets, – and yet…

And yet …As time passed, once Max the Judge's Associate moved on to becoming Max Sumner the successful barrister with constant work bringing in more and more money and much respect in the legal community and beyond, there was a feeling there should be more. A faint niggling question that he asked himself in the wee small hours– *was this all there was?*

Max started to contemplate what the next step in his career would be. He was certain that going to the bench and becoming a judge was not for him. It was too far removed from the cut and thrust of litigation, the challenge of using all his intellect and strategy to win a case - even more satisfying when the case appeared to be unwinnable. And besides, being a judge involved too much sitting down for him. All that bowing and scraping and purported respect. No, that was not for him. He craved more action and a closer connection to manipulating outcomes.

The more he thought about it the more he became convinced that the logical next step was to become involved in politics – Federal or State – either would do.

With his usual methodical approach Max set about ensuring this would occur. There was no rush. A successful outcome would only be achieved by careful strategic planning and then making his moves when the time was right.

Max took on more and more high-profile cases or represented clients who would be reported in the newspapers with the aim of building an acceptable media profile. The occasional pro-bono court appearance he knew was also worth doing, so long as they were ones that would attract public attention and were not too controversial. He didn't want to be categorised as a bleeding heart.

He accepted invitations to gallery openings, exhibitions, and concerts. He had always been in demand as an unattached man, good looking, charming, and young –but previously Max had declined all but the most appealing invitations. Now, with an agenda in mind Max exerted himself and turned on the charm whenever out and about in public, all the while keeping an eye out for those individuals whose friendship might prove to be useful and help him achieve his ambitions.

Being largely preoccupied with self-interest and his own needs Max was by and large apolitical. In his opinion all politicians were alike. If he was to progress with this plan of entering politics, he knew he would have to choose between any of the major parties. Representing an electorate as an independent or a member of a minor party was not for him. Too marginal. So, a major party it had to be. But which one? Liberal or Labor? Definitely not the Greens. Pragmatic as always Max knew he didn't have the passion for their brand of politics.

Opting for the Liberal Party was the rational choice. The Australian electorate it seemed to him was by and large instinctively conservative, and apart from the occasional surges to the left tended to favour the traditional liberal philosophies as a safe choice for the future. Decision made he commenced his research. In his usual methodical manner, Max identified those people who lurked in the background and were the real people of power. He then proceeded to make contact – discretely of course. He did not want them to realise they were being stalked. His hope was that these people, over discussions with colleagues, would share anecdotes about meeting a charming articulate and high-flying barrister who was making sounds about a new career in politics.

It was then that he realised that in order to succeed he needed to have a wife – and not just any wife. She had to be a wife from the right background and pedigree – intelligent of course, elegant, articulate and with her own career – so she would also attract media attention and thus promote his cause.

Max remembered the Judge's words about his daughter. Sabine. Not yet met but somehow Max knew she would be perfect.

# Chapter Twelve

# The young lawyer revisited

Another weekday, another workday and once again Sabine was running late for work. Racing along the inner-city streets on her bike she narrowly avoided several collisions with vehicles and irate pedestrians and somehow made it to work in one piece – hot and bothered, but fortunately unobserved by her supervisors.

'Where have you been?' asked Amy wrinkling her button nose in disgust as Sabine came close. 'And my, don't you smell awful!'

'Yeah. I know. And good morning to you too! Give me a minute. I'll have a quick wash in the downstairs shower and get changed. First, I'll just leave my jacket and handbag here, so it looks like I'm not far away. There – perfect!' Sabine said as she stood back to admire her work. 'I won't be long. This morning has already been a bit of a disaster. I slept in again!'

Sometime later a refreshed, and much more fragrant Sabine returned to her desk to find a steaming cup of coffee waiting for her.

'Amy you are a wonder. I owe you big time.'

'You certainly do. I just said you were in the Ladies. Rhys is after you.'

'I hope it's not that advice …again,' Sabine said with a grimace.

Smoothing her damp hair into a ponytail and after a quick slurp of her coffee she headed towards Rhys' office.

Rhys, head down focussed on a mass of documents, looked up at Sabine's hesitant knock.

'Ah, there you are. Good morning Sabine. More work for you here,' he said gesturing at the papers strewn across his desk. 'This one's a bit out of left field. I'm not sure what we will do with it, but it makes for interesting reading. That's for sure. Here you go, take all this back to your desk.'

He gathered the papers together and passed them over to her.

'And take this too.' Rhys reached into his Out Tray for a stapled document which he passed to her. With clenching stomach muscles, she recognised the document as being that dreaded draft advice. Surely, she didn't have to redo it – again?

'Just a couple of spelling mistakes but once fixed it is OK to go. Print that out as a final and I'll sign it. Well done Sabine.'

Sabine flashed a million-watt smile at Rhys as she accepted the papers. He started and gave her a surprised smile – a slightly puzzled expression on his face.

*Whoops. Tone it down Sabine. Be professional.*

'Thanks Rhys. What do you want me to do with these papers? Do I need to draft something?'

'Just read them for now. We have a meeting with the client this afternoon. About 2, I think. I'll make sure you are invited to the meeting.'

Struggling back to her desk, Sabine focussed on trying not to drop the bundle of assorted documents. With draft advice clenched between her teeth she was unable to respond to Amy whose head, once again like that of a prairie dog, had popped up above the partition and observed her approach with amusement.

'Well now. Looks like you have a bit to do. No more slacking off by arriving late,' she said with a smile.

Reaching her desk Sabine plonked down the papers then removed the draft advice from her mouth with a flourish and waved it above her head.

'Hurrah! It's done – finally. Not only am I allowed to print this off as a final – well after I've done a bit more fiddling that is, but Rhys actually praised me. He said *Well done*! Can you believe it? Finally.' Sabine's relief was obvious.

The advice finalised and left with Rhys' assistant Sabine settled down the read the papers. It was quite a mix – correspondence between various parties – letters and emails and a Will.... A Will?

The cover of this document displayed in large print a heading - *The Last Testament of Edmund Arthur McKay*. Whoever he was. Judging by the items bequeathed he was obviously someone of substance. The Will referred to several properties in the Eastern Suburbs, a farm in the Southern Highlands and numerous financial bequests to identified individuals some of whom were thanked for their loyal service. Employees Sabine assumed.

Once she had read the correspondence it became clear what this matter was about. A daughter Emma McKay had been omitted from the bequests, although the deceased had referred to her in the Will as a *'disloyal daughter not deserving of a share of my assets.'*

The correspondence was between Gemma and two people who appeared to be the Executors but could also be relatives given the shared McKay surname. Brothers perhaps? Whoever they were, one letter indicated in pompous tones that whilst they felt sorry for Gemma in her current situation, as Executors they felt bound to comply with the wording of the deceased's Will and were reluctantly unable to comply with her request. This letter signed *regretfully Charles and Phillip McKay.*

There was also a bundle of news clippings that contained details of the passing of Edmund McKay at the age of 85, a well-regarded industrialist and a scion of the squattocracy. His wife Enid long gone and survived by three children: two sons and a third child – a daughter. The sons – Charles and Phillip. Yes, she was right the brothers had been entrusted with the joint responsibility of being Executors of Edmund's will. According to the articles Gemma had always been a bit of a wild child – a successful career as a model and when Sabine considered the images reproduced in the clippings, even now as a woman who she thought must be in her fifties she still retained the fine bones and well-groomed appearance of a model. There were reports of an out-of-control drug fuelled lifestyle during her years as a model, two marriages, four children by four fathers and a long-standing estrangement from her father and brothers. It all seemed like something Sabine would expect to read in a weekly gossip magazine and not what she would expect to learn about at work especially in the hallowed halls of an establishment law firm such as *Smithtons*. At the very least it wasn't your run of the mill legal matter and certainly didn't promise to be boring.

Sabine made sure she was in place in the Boardroom well before the 2pm meeting, with notepad and the papers neatly placed before her. The Boardroom, a place only previously visited on the day of the graduate induction was a room that reeked of old money – dominated by an antique cedar table of mammoth proportions and what looked like significant oil landscape paintings adorning the walls which competed with but failed against the distraction provided by a sparkling Sydney Harbour vista visible through massive floor to ceiling windows.

The only other person in the room was Rhys' assistant who was busy placing a jug and four glasses on the table. Four people were to attend including her? Rhys and this new client Gemma McKay would be there but who was the fourth? That became obvious when the door opened and Fran appeared, looking slightly harassed and not her usual calm self. Dressed in her favoured severely styled suit but this time accessorised with a brightly coloured scarf tied closely around her throat. The bright colours of the scarf were a change to her usual subdued palette. Fran's hair curled softly to her shoulders. But a bright scarf and nicely styled hair could not detract from her drawn features and the dark shadows under her eyes. With a gentle smile she greeted Sabine.

'So, Rhys has drawn you into this matter. Families behaving badly. Rich or poor – it seems to happen everywhere. It happens more often when there's lots of money to fight over such as in this case and that seems to make such battles much more intense. And provides excellent fodder for the lawyers. Gemma McKay has been a client for years but usually it has been for more straightforward matters – divorces and house purchases. You will find her most interesting – trust me I'm not exaggerating,' said Fran with a grimace.

And that was no understatement. Shortly after Rhys appeared solicitously escorting Gemma into the Boardroom.

First impressions were of a tall, skinny scarecrow. Curly hair in wild disarray cascading around her shoulders. Baggy trousers on long, thin legs, a loose misshapen coat and a diaphanous scarf trailing behind her. Yet, despite her messy appearance Gemma made a strangely arresting sight. Closer inspection revealed an immaculately made-up face and impressive diamond stud earrings.

Introductions made, Gemma bestowed a brief smile on Fran and then her beautifully made-up eyes flickered in Sabine's direction – made an assessment, then moved on dismissing her as Gemma turned her gaze back to Rhys. Clearly Gemma was a man's woman.

'Thank you for seeing me so soon Rhys.' She spoke in the well-modulated voice of one who had been a product of private schooling, elocution lessons and privilege.

Gemma gestured at the papers on the Boardroom table. 'You no doubt have read all those and you can see I have been treated most unfairly by my father and now by both my brothers. All I am asking for is a share of the estate. There is so much to go around I cannot believe they would be so mean.'

Rhys reached for his notepad and pen. 'Gemma, do you mind if you give me some background as to your relationship with your father? Were you aware he intended to cut you out of his will? Had he provided for you in other ways?'

Gemma's eyes misted over as she recalled happier times when, as the only daughter she was cosseted and indulged by her father to the resentment of her brothers and possibly also her mother.

'My little Gem, he called me. Nothing was too much trouble. I was so much part of his life when I was growing up. I was the third and last child. Maybe my father felt like he had missed out when my brothers were young because he had been so busy becoming successful that when I finally arrived he found the time to focus on me. He would tell everyone how he delighted in being my father. He would take me everywhere with him. To meetings, site inspections – the lot. We had a special bond you see, and then it broke. I think that was because I failed to become what he wanted me to. You know I didn't want to go into the family business. Unlike my brothers, I wanted to make my own way, which I did. And I think he resented no longer having any control over me. Not that he ever said that outright. He had a way – you know of going all chilly and making it clear he didn't approve of my career and my lifestyle. But we still saw each other, and he made a point of being at my opening nights to celebrate my successes. Even in the bad times when I was admitted to rehab, he would be there to pick up the pieces.'

'Just to clarify, did he help you in other ways? You know financially?'

'Well, yes I suppose so. But then again, he helped my brothers as well. He helped each of us buy our first home. I never realised he held such resentment towards me. It came as a complete shock when dad was admitted to the hospice without me being informed. I tried to visit him there and was told he refused to see me. I was told it would be *too upsetting*. Too right! It was too upsetting for me! He was only in there for two days before he passed away – late diagnosis of pancreatic cancer you know. But I never got to say goodbye.'

At this, large tears welled in Gemma's eyes and rolled down her cheeks, her makeup remaining undisturbed, and the watery veil making her eyes glisten and look even larger. Sabine cynically watching this performance, despite herself felt rather impressed. Not many people could cry with such style. It took real talent.

Rhys put down his pen and reached behind to locate the box of tissues on the side table.

'Here please take a tissue. My apologies. I didn't mean to upset you. However, I do need to get some background details to see if there is any valid explanation as to why your father behaved as he did. If you are to proceed with your claim, we will need to prove that as his daughter you had a valid entitlement to part of the Estate. I see your brothers as Executors have turned down your request. So if you wish to take this further it would be necessary to bring the case before the court. But before doing that, you may wish us to write to the Executors on your behalf, giving them one more chance to settle part of the Estate on you before you start proceedings. Sometimes the threat of litigation can focus the thinking.' Rhys smiled gently at Gemma who was making subdued snuffling sounds into the paper tissue. Even that was done with style thought Sabine.

'I have a few more questions before we are done today. Then I and the team here will give some thought to the way forward which we will document in a written advice to you. If you decide to proceed further, we will need some written instructions from you. I would recommend we seek an opinion from a barrister as to your chances of success and maybe see how they would recommend proceeding. I know a suitable barrister with extensive experience in such claims. That may be worth considering – if that is what you wish?'

The meeting didn't continue for much longer. Once Rhys was satisfied that he had obtained sufficient information he smoothly wound-up proceedings and escorted his client from the room. Gemma left with a cursory wave in the direction of Fran and Sabine all the while talking to Rhys.

'Well, what did you make of that?' asked Fran with a grin and a roll of her eyes.

'I'm not sure. She is not what I was expecting as a client of this firm.'

'We've helped Gemma out before, so I suppose that's why she came to us. Most likely it won't be easy, as I imagine the brothers won't willingly hand over anything. But it could be an interesting matter, a change from the usual dry stuff we deal with.'

As she said this Fran pulled at her scarf as if it was hurting her and then with two hands untied and retied the scarf in what would be a more comfortable position. Fleetingly, so quickly that Sabine almost doubted what she saw was revealed a dark blotch on

Fran's neck that could only be a bruise. A million scenarios coursed through Sabine's mind as she tried not to show any reaction. Unlike a bruised shin, a bruised neck was unlikely to come about by accident. But was it appropriate to say anything given that Fran was now making such a fuss of rearranging her scarf to cover all? Fran after all was her boss and not someone she was close to.

Sabine resorted to babbling – about the client. 'You know I got the impression that Gemma McKay really only wanted to meet with Rhys and we two might as well have been invisible for all the attention she gave us.'

'Mmmm you're probably right and yet you and I will be the ones doing the hard work. Not that she will ever acknowledge it. That's just the way she is. And as our finance team would remind us, so long as she pays her bills what does it matter. We're not here to be her friends, just to help Gemma solve her problem.'

'I think I could take lessons from her in how to cry. I've never seen crying made to look so glamorous. It's hard to sympathise when I felt like I was watching a performance.'

'A performance -yes. Even so, it shouldn't detract from the reality that her father cut her out of his will. It seems mean when there is so much in that Estate to go around, but presumably the father really wanted to hurt Gemma. Some people carry hate to the grave.' Fran looked sombre as she said this.

Sabine saw her opportunity to pry and dived in:

'Fran you look sad. Are you OK?'

Fran gave herself a little shake as if coming back to the present.

'Thanks Sabine. Thanks for asking. I know I must look awful as I've had so little sleep – work and newborns are not a great mix. But I'm OK, I guess. It will pass.'

'If there's anything I can do, you'll tell me? Really, I mean it. I know nothing about babies, but if I can help with the work here, I'm happy to and that might give you a chance to leave for home early some nights. I can stay later. I only have a dog to walk and he can keep.'

'You are a dear.' This time Fran's smile was genuinely warm. 'I might take you up on that offer – then you'll regret it! Speaking of working late you remember the other night when I transferred my phone to you so I could get home in a hurry? I just remembered I hadn't checked with you if there were any calls. Did you take any messages?'

Sabine thought quickly. Somehow, she knew she shouldn't disclose being aware of the irate call from Fran's husband. If something was going on between Fran and her husband, she needed to build trust with Fran before she could be any help. And maybe consult with Stella – she had experience with domestic violence matters as part of her work as a Legal Aid solicitor. And Sabine was starting to suspect this might be what was impacting Fran.

'So sorry Fran. I think I might have missed a call. I was over at the photocopier when I heard my phone ring. By the time I got there it had stopped. It could have been a call for you – or me I suppose. I thought they might ring back, but when they didn't, I assumed it can't have been important. I checked the messages and there was nothing so I'm sorry if it then slipped my mind.'

'That's fine. As you say if it had been important, they would have rung back or left a message.' Fran looked almost relieved as she said this. Then gathering up her papers she stood, making it clear any further discussion between them was over.

\*\*\*

That evening over a shared meal of pizza with Stella Sabine recounted her day, starting with an elaborate description of the meeting with the new client and then outlining her concerns about Fran. Stella was most entertained by the description of Gemma.

'You know I have seen her photo in the social pages. She is such a beauty and seems to like going against the trend in her choice of attire. But somehow it suits her. There is always something happening to her – I guess that is why she is so beloved by the gossip columns. All those lovers, that tribe of children and certainly all those drugs! Yet she survives and some might even say she flourishes on all that controversy. Like someone out of a soapie.'

'But your Fran – now that's more concerning. If what you suspect is really happening, then that is a worry. For there is no guarantee she will flourish. Bruises on a neck are not a good sign – unless she is into some exotic sexual practices and I suspect with a newborn in the house, sex of any sort is out of the question.'

'But what can I do? I've offered to help with her office work. Stella I really need your wisdom and advice. This is so out of my life experience, and she is my boss – not my friend. I really feel constrained about what I can do – if anything.'

'Yes, it's not like anyone would try it on with you so you have no life experience to draw on. All I can suggest is that you be there for Fran. Keep an eye on her. If you notice any signs of distress or any further bruising, then I think it would be open to you to ask Fran if she is alright. But she needs to trust you. At this stage it seems like she is warming to you and in time she may come to see you as a friend. Given she is going to great lengths to act as if all is fine and keeping those bruises covered, I suspect she is not ready to open up about what is going on. That is if anything really is going on. We still don't know for sure.'

'You forget I heard him on the phone. Her husband sounds like a right cranky bastard, and a bully.'

'I get that. We know he is nasty and was making threats on the phone and we suspect she has been physically abused. Yet as you say Fran appears to be trying to carry on as if everything is as normal. I'll check our database and give you some phone numbers of organisations who can help Fran – that is if she wants to be helped. Don't forget it is up to her. You or anyone else can't save her. But if you see the chance to ask – the first thing to ask is if she -and her baby for that matter – feel safe. Give her the phone numbers I will write out for you and check if there are any family or friends who could help out. It's horrible I know, but family violence is everywhere.'

The two girls continued with their subdued eating – each lost in their own thoughts. Until Stella spoke: 'Don't think I can't see what you are doing? Since when was Grover entitled to pizza?'

'It's only the crusts. Go on, you wouldn't deprive this cute little starving third member of our household.' Sabine picked up her fluffy companion and waved his front paw at Stella. Grover meanwhile wiggled in Sabine's arms to get closer to the last remaining slice of pizza on the table.

Stella snorted. 'I give up. He can have that slice if he wants. I'm full and so should he be. Speaking of food are you and your precious dog up for Sunday lunch at my parents' house? Sam might join us – although that will depend on his work deadlines. Anyway, I'm sure my family would like to catch up with you and my nieces with Grover. My Nonna hasn't seen you for ages but she is bound to want to grill you about your marital prospects. That will take the pressure off me.'

'Lunch? Definitely! You're on. We'll both be there – won't we Grover. Grover?'

Grover was too busy gnawing on the last slice of pizza to pay any attention.

# Chapter Thirteen

# Sunday lunch

Stella's parents lived in Leichhardt, a suburb a short distance to the west of the Central Business District. It had been settled many decades ago by migrants from Italy and since then had become a bustling foodie hub. Stella's grandparents had settled there after they migrated to Australia in the 1950's when houses in Leichhardt were relatively cheap. Stella's parents lived just around the corner in a red brick house – just like so many built in that area. This was where Stella and her siblings had grown up. In a tight knit community where school was a short walk away, grandparents, aunts and uncles lived so close it almost felt like they were within shouting distance. And everyone in that connected community kept an eye out for each other. A very different upbringing to that experienced by Sabine.

It was a family tradition that every Sunday Stella's mother and her grandmother would cook the full-on Italian meal – soup and pasta to start with then followed by some sort of casserole of meats and vegetables that varied according to the season - more than enough to feed children, grandchildren and anyone else who cared to drop in. On special occasions such as birthdays, anniversaries, or any other occasion requiring celebration, even more food was prepared and the door was open to anyone who wished to share in the festivities.

This Sunday there was no particular reason to gather – no birthday and certainly no anniversary – it was just another Sunday afternoon spent at home. Yet even so the savory aromas of garlic, onion and herbs greeted them when they entered through the front door. The arrival of Stella, Sabine and Grover was always an occasion which generated much excitement. Grover bouncing around the two young children who were Stella's nieces, made it clear he remembered them and was happy to be back – but where was the cat? The cat with its instinct for self-preservation had already bolted outside, but its scent lingered and sent Grover into a frenzy of tracking.

Stella and Sabine headed to the kitchen after greeting Albie, Stella's father who was ensconced in the lounge room with Sunday paper on his knee and TV blaring in the background. The kitchen was located at the back of the house, down a long corridor off which various rooms and bedrooms opened. Reaching the kitchen was like entering into another fragrant and slightly steamy world. It was a large room – big enough for a table and opening onto a backyard that was mostly taken over by a sprawling vegetable garden and shadowed by a trellised grapevine growing over a pergola. By the stove a small elderly woman was focused on stirring something aromatic in a saucepan. But the real centre of activity was at the table where Stella's mother and her aunt were working quickly to shape pasta into small tortellini. The pasta was already rolled out. It was practised teamwork that clearly had been happening in this way for a long, long time. As quickly as Stella's mother Maria cut the dough into circular shapes, her sister dolloped a small spoon of a prepared filling into the centre and with skilful hands shaped and closed the dough around the filling, folding, pleating and securing each small bundle with a quick twist and then placing them on a tray that had been lined with non-stick paper.

Their arrival was greeted with smiles and exclamations.

'At last,' said Stella's aunt Elena. 'You can take over Stella while I toss a salad together. And Sabine, welcome my dear. Come here and give me a kiss.'

Sabine submitted to a slightly floury kiss then, as was always the case she was hugged and kissed in turn by Stella's mother and grandmother. Stella's grandmother or Nonna as she was called by everyone may have been given a name at her christening, but it was not known to Sabine. In all the years she had been visiting this family Nonna was all she had ever been called and so that is what Stella also called her.

Nonna was now in her eighties and it was beyond her comprehension that these two young women were still unmarried and childless. Of course, she was very proud of the university degree that her granddaughter had obtained and the successful career that had followed. But as far as she was concerned it would have been so much better if Stella had also acquired a husband when she was at university.

This Sunday commenced as it did every time they visited – with a cross examination by Nonna of both women regarding their romantic interests and marriage prospects.

'Don't laugh young ladies. You are not getting any younger. Your womb will dry up and soon it will be too late. I beg of you my granddaughter find a nice young Italian man and then I can die happy.'

Stella laughed as she patted her Nonna on her head. 'No rush – you have years to go. Maybe you need to find someone for me? Isn't that what loving relatives are supposed to do?'

# Chapter Fourteen

# Time for romance?

Two months had elapsed since her father's funeral and still the grief felt raw. Not just the feelings of loss but she also sensed a strange vacuum once filled by her father's presence. Previously her father had loomed large in Sabine's life – a voice guiding and directing her towards what he considered the correct choices for her – a career in law for instance, the *proper* friends and *appropriate* activities for a Judge's daughter to engage in. With his death there was no longer any such guidance in her life. The possibilities were now endlessly tempting, yet somehow terrifying.

Sabine was reluctant to share her feelings with anyone – least of all her mother who she still felt needed protecting. Apart from the exchange of a few brief text messages there had been no further contact between Sabine and her mother since the night of the ballet performance. Occasionally she would pause during her busy workday and wonder why she had not heard from her mother. Sabine would make a mental note to get in touch but then a deadline or urgent request would intrude, and that mental note would be lost in the chaos that was Sabine's thinking.

Time passed and it wasn't until late one Thursday evening that the mental note resurfaced. Immediately before she forgot – again – Sabine rang her mother who upon answering after several rings sounded breathless.

'Sabine dear. How lovely to hear from you, daughter dear. I was just thinking of you. How are things?'

'Me? I'm fine. It's just … well I was wondering how you were getting on as we haven't spoken for a while.'

'Ages?' Her mother paused as if considering the concept. 'Yes, I suppose that is correct. I've been busy and you probably have also – what with that demanding job and all.'

'I just thought I should check in and maybe come and see you. Sunday evening perhaps?'

Again, another pause, as if her mother was reviewing her busy social life to see if there was a vacancy. Her mother *never* had a busy social life. What was going on?

'Yeesss' said in a long drawl as if consideration was still being given to the possibility. 'Yeess. That should work. Why don't you come over about 6? I've something to show you and then we could walk down the road and get something for dinner at one of those trendy cafes you so love. No dog this time please.'

'OK ma. Fine. I'll see you then.' Sabine disconnected the call and stared thoughtfully at her phone as if that would clarify the mystery. What was going on with her mother? Why the mystery? Still a dinner was a dinner, and she was always up for a meal, especially at one of those places her mother loved to refer to as trendy – they didn't skimp on serving size and were not offended if she asked for a *doggy bag*.

Almost immediately her phone buzzed with a text message. Her mother? No. A quick glance revealed a message from Max. Sabine felt a bit embarrassed about how much use she had been making of him. How many times she had been disturbing him with what was most likely a stupid question or a request to review her draft advice. She knew she was taking advantage of him, but he was so polite and always seemed happy to help and it somehow made the task of navigating the challenges of *Smithtons* so much more bearable.

Sabine had tried on a number of times to express her appreciation, and each time it had been brushed aside with comments about how she was not alone in finding it confusing. He would reassure her by saying her experiences were nothing unusual and smile saying it was how we all went through this in the early days. Somehow, she doubted it. Sabine had regularly offered to buy him a drink or dinner as a way of saying thank you, but each time he was unable to accept because of court deadlines. Tonight, though he was free and was wondering if she would like to join him for a drink.

'Sure. My shout though. Where?'

They agreed to meet at a trendy bar not far from his chambers.

'If it's too crowded, we can go elsewhere. But it will do for starters.'

*Starters? What was he planning? A pub crawl? Or something more exciting?* Despite herself and as she remembered the frisson felt last time they met Sabine found herself hoping the evening might evolve into some other activities.

Crowded it was. After a quick scan of a room populated with legal types, all clad in their pin stripes or funereal black they decided to move on. Not before several people there had waved to Max.

'Let's go to the bar in one of the hotels nearby. Much more anonymous, and hopefully not full of legal types like here.

After the next bar was deemed unsatisfactory – too noisy – and as they continued down the road heading for Circular Quay Sabine started to wonder. Why the big deal? It was supposed to be just a drink after all. Was he always this fussy? She could sense his nervousness as he strode along. Even with her long legs Sabine found herself struggling to keep up

And anyway, she couldn't walk much further in these shoes. Big on style and a failure on comfort, her feet were now actively complaining.

As if sensing her pain Max turned to her.

'Sorry I didn't mean to drag you all over town like this. I just wanted to find somewhere cosy and not too noisy so we could have a chat.' He waved his arm in the direction of a well-known gourmet pub across the road. 'This will have to do. Let's hope there is a quiet corner inside where we can be heard.'

And to Sabine's relief there was. With a sigh she slipped off her shoes and surreptitiously gave her complaining feet a comforting rub while Max wandered over to the bar. No blisters – yet thank goodness – but she was definitely on for a cab ride home. The bike could stay at work for the night.

Conversation initially was a bit stilted and largely focussed on Sabine's experiences at *Smithtons*. At least she could be honest with Max. She was fairly certain he was not the type to blab.

'I guess it's not what I was expecting.'

'How so?'

'I accept that as a junior lawyer I have to start from scratch, but I didn't realise how tedious my work would be. Drafting and redrafting and rarely being allowed anywhere near a client. And if I am permitted to sit in on a meeting or a phone call then I am expected to sit in the corner like some naughty child. Sent to sit way down the back of the room and not permitted to say a word. I thought it would be more than this. I've spent over five years at uni and am being treated like I cannot be trusted. And so many people in the firm are downright unfriendly – not even a *Good Morning* when they walk past.'

'Maybe they're overworked and have no time for baby lawyers like you?' Max speculated. 'I really can't help you on that. I have never worked in a law firm so I cannot say whether all firms are the same or *Smithtons* is just unusual. As you know I went straight from uni to working for your father, and then to the bar. That was my career path and it suited me. Maybe you are discovering you are not on the career path that suits you?'

'You know that is exactly what Stella my flat mate said. You've met her – remember? Maybe that's it. But I feel like I should stick it for the graduate year until inspiration strikes.'

Their conversation moved on to what Sabine considered to be much more interesting topics– they talked about shared interests – food, theatre, the beach and books. It seemed to Sabine's delight that all of her interests were interests they shared. So many other times she had been down this path with other men to discover a dearth of connections. But this man not only looked good, was intelligent and understanding of her work issues, but also enjoyed the same interests in life as she did. Apart from his fixation in finding the perfect drinking venue he seemed ideal – almost too good to be true. But she was not going to reject him because of that.

They settled into a shared platter for dinner as both agreed it was too early to go home. And, as Sabine confessed there was nothing in the fridge at home to eat – apart from dogfood and she was not yet that desperate or that old to make dog food her dinner.

It was after 9pm by the time they had finished eating. Sabine after a quick glance at her watch gave a gasp. 'I must rush. I have to get home. There's a dog waiting for me – unfed and unwalked. He will be in mischief if I don't get home soon. Thank you, Max., It's been really lovely seeing you this evening. I know this was meant to be my shout but somehow, you've contrived to pay for everything. I still owe you. Maybe we can do this again next week?'

Max brushed her comments aside. 'I was happy to shout you this evening. You know it's not often I get time off to just sit around and talk about things other than the law. Such a welcome change. Too often I find myself working to all hours. It's not healthy I know but sometimes I feel like I'm trapped on a treadmill, and I really appreciate you dragging me away. I feel like I owe you.'

'No, no I owe you! Your patience in answering my silly questions and reviewing my endless draft advice. I would be lost without you.' As she said this Sabine had the dawning realisation that this could possibly be true. A not unwelcome thought – having someone in her corner was a new experience but something she thought she could get used to.

'Tell you what – seeing as we both are number one fans of each other - how about I prove my worth by cooking you something special for dinner one night? Clearly there is no point you cooking dinner for me as I seem to recall from that time I visited you have no food at home' This was said with a cheeky smile. 'What are you doing Saturday night?'

'Well, apart from grocery shopping – nothing.'

Arrangements made they left. Max to return to his chambers – something to finalise he said and Sabine with her sore feet ensconced in a cab speeding for home and a ravenous dog.

\*\*\*

By the time Saturday night came around Sabine was starting to feel nervous and wondered why on earth she had accepted a dinner invitation at Max's home. By going to Max's home would he automatically assume that she would be amenable to certain after dinner activities? It was so long since she had been actively involved in the dating game that she was not sure what was the expected protocol. When she confided her concerns to Stella she was no help at all. In fact, Stella found it hilarious and like Grover with his favourite toy, she would not leave the subject alone.

'Beanie, relax. You're overthinking things. He's gorgeous, single and obviously fancies you. He's being handed to you on a platter,' she said with a smile. 'What more do you want? It's just dinner and maybe if things go right a bit more. And if not? Well, you're a big girl – literally - and I'm fairly certain you can take very good care of yourself. But if you are concerned make sure you put my number on speed dial and give me the address. Go and enjoy yourself – I feel like I'm your mother or fairy godmother encouraging you to have fun. And most importantly what are you going to wear? Don't scoff – but maybe it should be something easy to remove if you do get carried away! And don't wear your usual daggy underwear!'

Much thought was given to what to wear to dinner with Max. In the end and after a number of outfit changes supervised by a puzzled Grover who sadly recognised *going out without the dog* clothes, she decided on a simple maxi sun dress in a blue and green floral print. That afternoon was still late autumn warm but with the promise of a cool evening to come. Sabine packed into her tote bag her favourite blue cardigan along with a bottle of what the local wine shop described to her as an outstanding Pinot Noir and some chocolates.

Max lived in an apartment at Potts Point, not that far from her home in Darlinghurst but too far for her to walk that evening. Stella had offered to give her a lift which Sabine declined knowing full well that Stella had plans of her own. She was being secretive about who she was going out with but judging from the care Stella was also taking with her appearance the outing could also be significant.

'Do tell. What are you doing tonight? And who are you seeing? I've told you all, so it is now your turn.'

'Nothing to tell yet. Although…' Stella smirked. 'I do have hopes. Call me superstitious. I just don't want to jinx it.'

'Well superstitious. Does the person for whom you are going to all this trouble happen to be a certain young journalist called *Sam*?'

Stella's expression was response enough. That and the pillow she hurled in Sabine's direction. With a laugh and a wave Sabine exited the room and the house – but not before giving a disconsolate Grover a chewy doggy treat, which went some way to cheering him up. For ten minutes at least.

Max lived in an apartment block in a secluded leafy street in Potts Point. Not an enormous apartment block – maybe three or four storeys and judging by the dark red brick detail and the grand entrance porch flanked by pillars it was possibly a building with an Art Deco inspiration.

Pressing the bell next to Max's name she was buzzed through multi-paned glass doors into a gracious entry – tiled in black and white tiles and with high ceilings, the cornice profile detailed in a staggered geometric shape that confirmed Sabine's guess as to the age of the building.

Eschewing the easy option of taking the lift Sabine strode towards the stairs which curved up from the centre of the foyer. By the time she reached the third floor she was puffing and didn't present her hoped for elegant appearance to the man quietly standing by an opened door.

'Welcome. There is a lift you could have used or are you trying to work up an appetite?' Max's eyes twinkled his good humour. Dressed in faded blue jeans and a checked shirt he looked much more elegant than Sabine now felt.

'Never have to work up an appetite. My dad used to say the only time I wouldn't be hungry was when I was dead.' A shadow passed over Sabine's face as she remembered that such words would never again be said. A sympathetic look from Max greeted her comment and as if in understanding he pulled her close and following a quick peck on her cheek he ushered Sabine into the apartment.

Max's apartment was one of two apartments occupying the third floor and, of course, occupied that side of the building that benefited from sweeping harbour views.

Walking past Max Sabine in one glance took in the open-plan living area which looked out onto a wide balcony. To one side of the room was a sleek kitchen – all white cupboards and marble benchtops. Preparation for dinner was spread out on the marble topped kitchen island. A glass dining table was centred in the room, and on the far side, two lounges faced the TV installed on the far wall. Contemporary paintings in bright colours were displayed on the wall on either side of the entrance and bright rugs completed the modern décor. Out on the balcony she could see further groupings of seats and a BBQ.

'Wow this is amazing.'

'Yes, it is,' Max smiled in agreement. 'It took me a while to find it but it is everything I want. Two bedrooms down there.' He pointed towards the door to the right of the TV. 'And the bathroom is also down that corridor if you need it.'

He steered Sabine towards the kitchen bench where two glasses and a bottle of champagne stood in readiness beside a platter of fruit, various types of cheeses and cracker biscuits.

'Fancy a pre-dinner drink? I thought we could enjoy the sunset out on the balcony and then I have some meat and vegetables to BBQ. It's all pretty straightforward but you can help me with that if you wish – or you could supervise? OK with Champagne?'

'Of course.' Sabine was never one to refuse a drink – especially French Champagne.

Oiled by food and drink they settled into an easy conversation of people who by now had some familiarity with each other. They marvelled over how the roof tops below faded into insignificance when the distant outlook of harbour with its associated activities and landmark constructions were observed. The screech of cockatoos and chatter of parrots in nearby trees competed for attention.

'So much wildlife here in the inner city. Who would have thought it?' exclaimed Sabine.

Just you wait until dusk. Then you will see clouds of flying foxes flying out from the Botanic Gardens over there.' Max pointed down and to the left. 'And of course, there will be the occasional possum running along our balcony – looking for leftovers, I suppose. I often sit out here in the evenings. It's so restful you see.'

After two glasses of champagne each and fuelled by snacks Max decreed it was time to start cooking. Dinner was simple he explained. "I'm really not much of a cook as you will soon see.'

Main course was simple. He had already prepped the steak in a red wine marinade. Sliced zucchini and asparagus spears which he planned to char grill on the BBQ – probably first steamed before he started to cook the meat.

'So they can come to room temperature and I will then dress the vegetables in some olive oil before I give them a quick char grill for further flavour – and a sprinkling of salt and pepper maybe.'

'Sounds perfect to me.'

And it was. They sat outside on the balcony and in between mouthfuls of delicious food and even more champagne they chatted and chatted. Meanwhile the evening settled in around them. The afterglow from the sunset lit up the nearby buildings in a rosy hue. The harbour bridge stood out in dark relief against the fading sky. With a cacophony of screeching the flying foxes left their daytime resting places and took to the air in a darkened mass. Max pointed at them.

'See – there they go. Off for their evening meal. Every evening it's like this – and there in the background you can hear another screech – that's from the cockatoos. I like to watch the transition to evening – when I'm home that is, and not at work. It reminds me that this city is so much more than just us humans and how it is also home to other forms of life. Possibly more interesting ones at that.'

Sabine comfortably full of food and champagne nodded. There really wasn't much to say but agree. They sat for a while in comfortable silence as the evening settled in around them. Gradually the lights of the city came on – shining into the night sky and reflecting on the harbour. Max reached out to Sabine and helped her to her feet.

'I think it's time to come inside away from the mosquitos and maybe I can tempt you with a coffee?'

Still holding her hand Max pulled Sabine closer and kissed her gently on the cheek. His touch, his warm slightly toasty smell was enticing - luring Sabine to lean in – to rest her cheek on his chest and breath in. Then, almost without conscious thought she lifted her face and ….

Kissing, more kissing and murmuring from Max.

'You don't know how much I have wanted to do this. Ever since we first met. To kiss you - here and here.' The lightest of kisses on her throat, her chest and returning up to her lips where the kisses increased their intensity. Sabine found herself responding and with increasing passion her hands explored Max. The strong back muscles usually hidden under barrister robes or a suit were now revealed to her questing fingers. She liked the way his back narrowed down to a tightly muscled bum which she tentatively cupped with both hands and then pulled him in closer to her. Max was only slightly taller than her, so it was immensely satisfying to grind herself into Max and feel his physical response. All the while kissing and groaning. Then with a gasp Max pulled free.

'This is all going a bit fast. Are you sure you want to continue?'

'Oh yes, yes,' groaned Sabine lost in the heat of passion. What she wanted was clear to her. She didn't want him to stop. The sensations flooding her had not been felt for some time. A bit of a man drought had put paid to that. And it seemed to her that this man knew how to press her buttons.

Taking her by the hand Max led Sabine through the living room, down the corridor and into a bedroom. Even in the throes of passion Sabine observed how tidy this room was – more like a hotel room. Devoid of personal touches. No framed photographs. One landscape painting hanging above the bed and two bedside tables with a lamp on each – nothing else. No books, no detritus of daily life – nothing. But then the present intruded as Max gently undressed her – starting at the top. Kiss, unbutton, kiss, remove shirt, kiss, undo bra, kiss and suck, and kiss down on her tummy as he gently pushed her onto the bed. Kiss and more kiss as shoes and trousers removed. Kiss and kiss along thighs and around the outline of her black lacy knickers. As he went to remove said knickers, Sabine held up her hand.

'No. No you don't. No more. Not until you remove some of your clothes. Fair's fair. Why should you have all the fun. Now strip!'

Of course, ma'am. As you command,' he smiled and with the practised moves of a stripper and associated humming Max divested himself of all clothes and slowly turned around for the inspection by the stunned lady sprawled on his bed.

'Like what you see?'

Sabine took in the glory of this burnished and muscled young man.

'Oh yes.'

Nothing more was said and indeed nothing more was necessary as, once a condom was located and put on, they settled into the lovemaking moves that have been around for eons. Thrust and counterthrust they breathed in unison, sighed and gazed into each other's eyes, as passion exploded and then left them spent.

'That was amazing,' purred Sabine. Then: 'can you do it again?'

'You are such a demanding woman,' groaned Max as he reached for and kissed the back of her hand. 'Give an old man a break. If you are so keen, maybe you should entertain me?'

'Now there's a thought,' Sabine smiled. 'Give me a moment to go get us some more champagne and then maybe I can think of something…'

\*\*\*

Shards of sunlight penetrated Sabine's confused dreams and roused her to consciousness. A momentary panic when, opening her eyes, she found herself in an unfamiliar room with a body lying next to her quietly snoring. Then realisation dawned, as with quiet contentment she reviewed the events of last evening and concluded that all had been satisfactory with the potential for an interesting future. Sabine leaned on one elbow and contemplated the man at rest beside her. Max sound asleep looked very different from the ever-alert awake Max. Softer, more vulnerable maybe – his face settled in gentle repose – relaxed and at peace. If this was the real Max she found herself liking him even more. The Max that she was coming to know not only was easy on the eye, ever helpful and accommodating of her stupid legal questions, but last night he had proved himself to be a most satisfactory lover. Considering all their intimacies last night possibly even more than satisfactory!

Giving a little snort Max stirred and rolled towards her reaching out with a questing arm. A sleepy eye half opened and squinted in Sabine's direction.

'Good morning' he smiled, as he gently ran his hand down Sabine's side. 'How are you beautiful one? Slept well, did we?'

'Like a log! Must have been all that champagne.'

'Definitely,' he smirked and in response, received a knowing smile from Sabine as she leaned in to kiss him.

Sometime later, the realities of life intruded on Sabine's thoughts. She sat up with a rush.

'I must go.'

'Go? What? Where? Why?'

'My dog Grover. He is at home and will need walking. It's Sunday, and Stella my housemate will be with her parents for their weekly luncheon frenzy. Grover is on his own and will need to get out before he gets into mischief.'

'Grover? He's just a dog. He can keep. Surely you have more important things to do here?' His eager hands continued their exploration of Sabine's body.

*Just a dog?* Sabine stiffened as the intent behind those words registered. Just when she was starting to think this man might be special, he then lobbed in this grenade.

'I really *must* go. Dog or not. Grover is my responsibility,' she said, launching herself from the bed. With questing hands Sabine grabbed her clothes which had been scattered in all directions around the room and began to frantically get dressed.

Too late, Max realised his mistake. He could almost see the determination radiating from the woman who was, by now almost fully dressed and would shortly bolt out of his apartment and possibly from his life. He knew he could not allow that to happen – not when he had their future together so perfectly plotted out. He had to act – now!

'Sabine. I'm sorry that came out all wrong.' Bounding out of the bed and approaching Sabine he gently drew the stiffening woman to him. 'I am really sorry,' he repeated, as if repetition would make it right. 'I was being selfish and wanting you all to myself. That was wrong. Your dog is important and maybe I can help? Please?'

He could feel her resistance softening. Maybe all was not yet lost?

'Perhaps we can both walk young Grover. Take him to Centennial Park and also try out the café there. Skip breakfast here and have brunch after we walked the dog. I SO don't want us to end today on a bad note. Forgive me?' Max smiled in what he hoped was a winning way.

Well, it was possibly understandable that Max had yet to understand the bond between a pet owner and their dog, thought

Sabine. After all he had no pets and as far as she was aware had never had any animals to care for. Perhaps she should give him the benefit of the doubt and not end the relationship before it had even had a chance to start. The old Sabine would have stormed off in a huff, but she liked to think the new mature Sabine, she was evolving into since her father's death, might be more understanding of others – showing some empathy and perhaps giving Max the chance to make amends.

But then again – no! If he didn't like dogs, then Max was not the one for her. The new evolved Sabine was not so understanding after all.

'No Max. Not today. I think Grover and I need to be on our own.' She couldn't resist continuing with a dig – and why not. 'I'm not sure Grover would appreciate being considered *just a dog.*'

Holding up her hand as Max went to speak, she added 'You're entitled to your opinions. Just give me some time. I'll contact you later.' And remembering her manners: 'Thanks for last night. It was – interesting.' With a wave and a smile, she turned on her heels – left the room and the apartment - leaving Max lost for words and wondering how he had got it all so wrong.

By the time she and Grover had power walked around Centennial Park and refuelled at a café on the way back home Sabine had calmed down. Maybe she had overreacted – but Grover was special to her. A small puppy rescued from the dog foster home; he had quickly evolved into her best friend – apart from Stella that is. *Love me love my dog* was very much on her mind as Sabine turned the corner into her home street and saw Max leaning against the metal railing peering intently down at his phone. It appeared to her that he may have been waiting for some time. His body slumped in dejection gave a clue to how he was feeling. Grover, traitor that he was, saw Max and giving a welcoming bark raced ahead to this person who he recognised. Max, pocketed his phone, bent down and welcomed him with open arms – fussing and rubbing the ecstatic pooch.

Typical, Sabine thought. That wretched dog was clearly indiscriminating and no judge of who should be his real friends.

As she approached, Max paused in the rubbing of said pooch's ears and looked up at her.

'Forgive me? Your dog certainly has,' as Grover nudged Max urging him to continue with the ear rub.

Despite herself Sabine found she was smiling in response. It took too much effort to hold a grudge, especially after last night. There really was incentive to give Max another chance.

Opening the gate, she waved Max in. 'Forgiven – for now. But watch your step.' She smiled. 'My dog is part of the package – understood?'

'Understood,' he said meekly.

Over a coffee they both worked hard to repair the rift. It was such a balmy afternoon that they decided to sit outside in the compact brick paved courtyard with Grover sprawled on the ground below them soundly asleep, his head resting on Max's feet. Their conversation initially stilted, expanded as they regained their ease with each other. Sabine confided in him about her concerns about her mother, and how she had been summoned to see her that night.

'That's not like my mother to issue an order to attend. She is usually much more restrained than that. It was dad who nearly always gave the orders. I suppose she is having to evolve. I haven't seen her for a few weeks. Work has been all consuming and I'm kind of concerned that something might have happened. Maybe she is ill or …I don't know - she just sounded so strange on the phone the other night that I can't help worrying.'

Max reached out and clasped her hand in both of his. Her hand, large and perfectly shaped for handling basketballs felt strangely dainty when held this way. And safe. And protected.

'It's OK to worry. Especially after everything you and your mother have been through following the loss of your father. Maybe she has something good to share? Whatever it is, I'm home tonight and please – come and see me afterwards if you want – or call if only to debrief.'

The sound of the front door slamming, jerked Grover awake and with a cacophony of barks he raced inside.

'That will be Stella back from her weekly family get together. I warn you her mood can be dangerous depending on how much she has been harangued by her mother and grandmother.'

Today, however must have been a good day, as the Stella that emerged from the back door together with frisking dog was all smiles.

'Oh, hi Max. Hi Beanie. You missed a great meal. Everyone was asking after you. Maybe next time you should bring Max? That would get them off my back!'

After Max left, Stella pulled up a chair and with a penetrating look spoke:

'OK Beanie. What gives? You have that *loved up* look, yet you look strangely subdued. So not you. If there has been a wonderful night of passion how come you are not bouncing off the walls? Do share with your Aunty Stella,' she smiled encouragingly.

'Yeah, to loved up – *really* loved up. And I think I should be bouncing – it's just we had a little spat – a difference of opinion over Grover, and I stormed off. It seemed like a deal breaker at the time, but I think we have now sorted it out. I think we both want to continue with whatever we have started.'

'A bit more detail - on the spat please, not the loved-up bit. Let's just leave that part to my imagination.'

'Well… it's like this…'

A few minutes later Sabine drew breath and looked at Stella expectantly, waiting for her judgement on the events.

'Beanie. You hardly know each other. If you see a future with this man this might be the start of many such misunderstandings that you will need to work through. Work through like the mature responsible adult you are. Now don't roll your eyes. Sounds like he has apologised and is prepared to make amends. Grover you say - likes him?'

'He's no judge of character, that one. He even likes the postman.' Reaching across and giving Stella a hug, Sabine continued: 'Darling Stella what would I do without you – full of wisdom as always.'

'I can sort out your life. But I sure as hell can't sort out mine. My love life is a disaster. I thought there might have been something developing with Sam. But no. Wrong again. He just wants to be *friends*!' With a scream that was half anguish, half hysterics Stella's voice rose several octaves until she and her best friend collapsed in squeals of laughter and a small dog scampered away from these dangerous humans and back inside the house to safety.

# Chapter Fifteen

# Dinner with Anna

From the very start Sunday evening with her mother was just plain weird.

'I thought we might stay in after all,' her mother said after greeting Sabine with a gentle kiss and hug. 'That way we can have a proper talk and not be rushed out of the restaurant just because they want to allow time for a second sitting.'

*A proper talk?* Since when had her mother cared for such things?

Her normally calm and serene mother was virtually fizzing with excitement. No calm measured steps gliding around the kitchen as was her usual practice. This night she fussed and skittered to and fro, fretting over this and that – her behaviour consistent with that of someone preparing an important entry for a major cooking competition and not just another Sunday night dinner with her only child.

'Ma don't fuss so. Let me help.' Sabine wondered if this buzzing was a sign of her mother having something to share – something to make her so excited – a romance perhaps? But with whom? All her mother's so-called friends were friends of Sabine's father and in her opinion – old, doddery and past it.

It wasn't until after dinner had been eaten and they were engaged in a token argument over chocolate choices from the box of chocolates Sabine had brought with her that Anna explained the cause of her happiness. But not before taking care to set the scene. Her nervousness apparent by the fidgeting hands and the way she carefully took her time to get to the point. It took so long that in the end Sabine snapped:

'Ma out with it. Are you ill? Have you taken a lover? If it is the latter, I won't mind – dad is gone after all. If you are ill – now that is another matter, and I will always be there for you. But this tippy toeing around the subject is just filling my head with all sorts of speculation and dread. Please put me out of my misery. Tell me now. Or I shall scream!'

Her mother had listened to Sabine with what was clearly an expression of amazement and then with a look of amusement she spoke.

'My dear neither of those things. Although maybe a lover one day might be tempting. That is if anyone would ever fancy a dried-up old prune like me.'

'Ma you're gorgeous. How many times are you mistaken for my older sister? It's really quite heartbreaking for me. But anyway – do tell. So, if it's not any one of these scenarios, what is it. Spit it out.'

'Dear – language. Remember you are a lady. And no need to snort. What I have to tell you is rather exciting. Or at least I think it is.'

'Well, I won't know how exciting it is if you don't tell me!'

'Alright, alright. It's a bit of a story – and grunting at me in that manner won't make me rush. Since your father died, I've been doing a bit of thinking.'

'And me too. So?'

'Well, a lot of thinking – actually. I'm still quite young – wrinkled old prune that I may be, and I realised that things must change if I'm to enjoy the rest of my life. So much of how I used to live – the charities, this house and all those functions were important to me because they were important to your father. Now that he is no longer with us I see no need to continue as I did. With that in mind I took action and I have resigned from various charities. That was easy and I did it soon after your father's death.

In fact, I think people seemed to expect me to do that. There was no need for lengthy explanations.'

'That makes sense. You used to moan about all those meetings and the power plays of various people. Do continue. I sense there is more?'

Her mother nodded. 'So correct my dear. There is. I then decided it was time to move away from here. One little old person does not need to live in this enormous house. I always felt it wasn't a place you would eventually return to. Yes, I see you nodding. There really is no need to keep it and I kind of liked the idea of living in something smaller – an apartment maybe? With a garden on a balcony and maybe two bedrooms – one for me and one for you when you visit. Nothing fancy. And anyway …apparently this place is worth a lot of money – or so I'm told.'

Drawing a deep breath Anna, stared intently at her daughter as if to judge her reaction and launched into what she had really been concerned about.

'So, I've sold it.'

'Sold it? But I haven't seen a *For Sale* sign out the front or read any advertising.'

'That's right. Sold off market without even being listed. I spoke to two different Real Estate firms who couldn't have been more helpful. One had two different purchasers who were keen – awfully keen really and it sold last week for more money than I would ever have thought possible. Even after I use some of the proceeds to buy an apartment, I will still have quite a bit to invest. What with that and your father's pension I can manage quite comfortably. It's quite a good outcome – a very good outcome actually. Now that the contracts have been signed and exchanged, I feel quite relaxed – like a weight has been lifted from my shoulders.'

Her mother paused then continued after she noticed Sabine's stunned expression.

'Sabine dear don't stare at me like that. It's not too complicated – really.'

Sabine was not sure what to think. This decisive person in front of her talking about making such life changing decisions was not a mother she recognised. The mother she grew up with could never have unilaterally spoken to agents and sold her home without weeks, months even of indecisiveness and extensive consultation. Had her father's death brought about this change in personality?

She gazed thoughtfully at her mother, whose hand hovered indecisively over several chocolates. Unable to make a decision about which chocolate to select, but able to sell her home without a qualm. What a contrast!

'Ma. I'm lost for words. And yes. Don't laugh. I agree that very rarely happens.' Sabine drew breath as she groped for something to say, 'but ... well done you. Congratulations. If this is what you want to do, then I'll fully back you. I never really liked this house anyway, although I suppose I have lots of happy memories of growing up here.'

'You didn't like it?'

'Nah. Too showy. The pool – now that I loved. I'll miss swimming there – and the view too I suppose.' Sabine paused as a thought struck her: 'What about my uncle? Have you told him?'

Sabine was aware that her uncle, her father's brother was almost as controlling as her father – as his behaviour had demonstrated not that long ago at the funeral when he shepherded Anna around just like a determined sheep dog.

Anna grimaced as decision made, she dived and secured the last chocolate ginger in the box while swatting her daughter's hand away.

'Ouch! What a bully I have for a mother.' Sabine peered closely at her mother. 'Let me guess. You've yet to tell him? Are you scared of him?'

'Mmmm not exactly. It just seemed easier to present him with a fait accompli. He and your aunt are going overseas this week for a holiday so I think I might leave telling them until they return. I wouldn't want to spoil their holiday.' The last sentence said with false concern as mother and daughter shared knowing smiles. Concern for Sabine's uncle had never been their shared motivation.

'It can wait. By the time I tell them both I will have moved to Melbourne and will be well and truly settled in my new life.'

Sabine shook her head as if there was something she was mishearing – that or her ears had been blocked.

'Come again. Melbourne?'

'Sabine. Keep up. It's not that complex. Listen carefully now. I'm selling up – well to be more accurate I have sold. Next week I will visit Melbourne for a few days and look at apartments to rent. I plan to rent for 6 months. That will give me time to scope the town and decide which would be the best area to buy in. I have a few ideas, but it's best to actually spend time living there before making a decision.'

This couldn't be happening. Her oh so sensible mother leaving town just like that – on a whim almost and moving to a city she knew nothing about. She knew that Anna had done her ballet training in Melbourne years ago – but that was almost a different life. Not only had Anna changed, but the city certainly would have.

'But why Melbourne?'

Her mother stared at her daughter in astonishment.

'Isn't it obvious? It's where the ballet company is based. Andre says there will be role for me somewhere – certainly as a volunteer to start with and if I focus on getting my teaching qualifications, I will be able to help with the adult beginner ballet classes they run for the public. And I'm hoping I might be able to participate in the company classes – and perhaps mentor some of the young dancers. Andre thinks I could be quite useful – *inspirational* even he says,' said Anna, her excitement palpable.

'So, this is Andre's idea?'

'Not just his. We both talked about it. Quite a bit actually.'

Anna explained how after their evening at the ballet all those weeks ago she and Andre had kept in regular contact – even meeting on the occasions when Andre happened to be in Sydney. It didn't take long for them to re-establish their old rapport. Andre listened while Anna grappled with what to do with her life now that her husband was no longer there to take control. Initially he kept silent as he sensed Anna needed time to process her thoughts to determine what path to take. Andre already had ideas of his own, but he knew how to be patient. After all he didn't want to assume the role previously filled by the Judge – the role of manipulating Anna's life. With a bit of care, he thought he could still achieve the outcome he desired without any direct influence. So, to start with Andre had listened and when it was his turn to speak, he contented himself with sharing with Anna his day-to-day concerns – the issues with the dance company, the ever-constant financial constraints and the artistic direction he wished to steer the company in over coming years. Financial constraints he was fairly sure would be of no interest to Anna – important though they were – but discussion concerning artistic direction and temperamental dancers he was sure would intrigue her. And they did. It didn't take long for Andre to entice Anna and lure her in. For it was obvious by the interest she showed in these regular confidences that Anna was discovering how much she had missed her artistic life. Something she now shared with her daughter.

'Sabine my dear. I don't expect you to understand but I now feel like I've rediscovered a part of me that I had thought I had lost a long time ago. I had always felt like I couldn't go back to the life I used to lead all those years ago and that I would have to settle for being content with my lot. Not that it was too bad. But now Andre has convinced me that it is still possible to be involved in my craft and not just in a token way. I feel like I've been reborn. I'm so excited. Be pleased for me. I know you have your own life, but I hope you will still consider wherever I choose to live will also be your home. Of course, you have your home here in Sydney and I would never choose to sell that out from under you. But maybe in time you may choose to live somewhere else.'

Sabine stared blankly at her mother.

'Don't grump at me dear. But I do wonder if this life you are currently living is one of your own choosing or one your father chose for you?'

It was all too much. Not only was her mother abandoning her, but she was also reminding her that the roof over Sabine's head belonged to her mother and could be at risk of being sold. Given her mother's recent actions in precipitous selling it could be that the first she might hear of a sale was the arrival of the new owners. It didn't bear thinking about. And now her mother was offering career advice? Just because her mother had been fortunate enough to rediscover her vocation that didn't make her an expert on what would suit her daughter.

There was way too much to process. Especially after all that had happened today. A glance at her watch confirmed the hour was late enough for her to leave without causing suspicion.

'Ma. I'd better go. It's a workday tomorrow and all that. No, don't see me out. I know the way. Give me a hug.' Sabine leant down to envelop her dainty mother in an embrace. A bit like an elephant cuddling a mouse she thought as she felt her mother's slight frame. Taking her mother's hands, she looked down and peered into those dark velvety eyes that she so wished she had inherited. So mysterious and so much more enticing than the almost transparent blue eyes gifted to her by the Judge.

'I'm really pleased for you ma. I am – really. Surprised. Stunned even. I didn't know you had it in you. But I'm there right behind you. Such an inspiration you are. And I'll certainly help you sort and pack up this stuff when it's time to move. And if I'm brave enough I'll be there to pick up the pieces when you tell all to my uncle. Now that will be interesting.'

\*\*\*

Later that night as she lay in bed Sabine mentally reviewed the discussion with her mother – occasionally sharing choice titbits with the canine snuggled next to her.

'You know Grover. I feel almost envious of ma – yes surprised that she could suddenly ditch her old life without a qualm, but also slightly resentful that she is so excited about her future – like it is a dream come true.'

Grover, sensing a response was required, licked at the hand that was thoughtfully patting him. Then as the hand stilled, he nudged her to continue.

'It's not that I want a career in ballet. Imagine an elephant like me cavorting around the stage! But somehow – I wish I could be a bit more excited about what I'm currently doing. Max says give it time – but really Grover. How much time do I have to give it?'

Feeling his mistress was again seeking a response Grover reached up and licked her chin. Somehow that would just have to do.

# Chapter Sixteen

# Sabine the young lawyer in love

The following few weeks settled into a pattern. Up early to walk the dog, rushing to work, late as always, then days of deadlines, meetings and on some evenings, time was spent with Max. Sabine was coming to realise that Max as a successful barrister was often very busy. She tried not to resent those last-minute phone calls, the cancellations of prior engagements and the fulsome apologies for his inability to meet her for dinner. As if in recompense he would then offer the olive branch of an early breakfast at their favourite café. Disappointing – yes – but not surprising. Growing up as a child of a judge and having experienced her father's long working hours she knew how pressured and unpredictable a life in litigation could be. Sabine tried not to feel too annoyed about the regular cancellations and abject apologies, yet sometimes it was hard not to feel like she was being taken for granted.

Occasionally she would stay over at his place, more than not this happened on the weekends when life was more leisured. He had stayed once at Sabine's house which had turned out to be slightly challenging. She soon discovered that Max did not like sharing the bed with a small dog. And to Sabine's surprise, a certain dog was also not too keen on sharing a bed with Max. Sabine recognised this situation would have to be resolved if they were to make long term plans for an ongoing relationship, but at this early stage she decided it was better to keep the peace, spend more money on the dog walker and stay over at Max's place.

Apart from the dog issue everything else seemed perfect. Spending time with Max was like putting on a comfortable slipper – somehow feeling exactly right - welcoming and so relaxing. And at times even better than relaxing. Max the lover was – well, almost perfect. Considerate of her needs but also demanding – yet with his own passion, able to kindle her response to heights Sabine had never before experienced. She found herself wanting more – and perhaps it was because of this Sabine found herself feeling so let down when Max would once again cancel giving as a work deadline as a reason.'

It wasn't as if she was some pathetic woman sitting at home waiting for a call. No. She was a dedicated career woman – busy with work deadlines of her own – and if she needed social interaction – well there were always her girlfriends with whom to socialise. Sabine found herself explaining this to Stella one night after Max had once more changed arrangements – ringing with profuse apologies to say he could no longer make that evening's planned get together, but at least offering as an alternative an early breakfast the next day at the café near his work.

'It's not that I don't understand how demanding his work is. I do. And of course, my work hours are also incredibly unpredictable – as are yours Stella. But this constant change to prior arrangements is starting to get me down. It's bringing back memories from my childhood when ma and I never knew what time dad would get back home. All those evenings ma and I spent sitting at the table, having dinner together without him and my being long in bed long before I would hear dad return. Sometimes I would wonder if dad's work was the real excuse or if there was some other woman in his life – and now I'm starting to feel the same way about Max.'

It was clear Sabine was distressed. She was sitting slouched at the kitchen table – cup of tea gripped by tensed hands. Her eyes, normally shining clear and bright were now watery with unshed tears. A frown as she pondered her misery, and a pursing of lips made her face almost unrecognisable. Stella realised she had to act, or her dear friend would be wallowing in misery all evening and that would just cast a gloom over the entire household. It was time for diversion therapy.

'Come on Beanie. No more misery guts. You are a grown woman and in charge of your own destiny. There is a city out there waiting for us – countless bars and bistros in our neighbourhood – just steps away. How about I text Sam and see if he is able to join us and we will go and celebrate.'

'Celebrate? What exactly?'

'Maybe our good fortune to live in this city, to know each other and – I don't know – just because we can. Come on, get your jacket and let's go. Your dog has been fed and there is no reason to stay at home and mope. Look – Sam just texted back. He says he can join us shortly. After he's finished whatever article he's currently working on. What about we check out that bar that's just up the road? The new one?'

The bar was only two blocks away – in what was once a corner shop but had since been repurposed into a cosy bistro – with a courtyard garden out the back and tables spilling out onto the front pavement. They found a tiny table inside by the front window that was being vacated as they arrived. Sabine with the speed of long practice dashed across and claimed the table before anyone else could. Her agility and speed from all those years playing netball once again coming to the fore. Stella recognising her role was to procure drinks and sustenance, squeezed between the groups at the bar and gave her order.

By the time Sam arrived they were settled, sipping their drinks of choice – a cocktail for Sabine and a glass of white wine for Stella and surveying a wooden platter strewn with assorted dips and other antipasti items.

'Perfect timing Sam,' said Stella greeting Sam with a quick kiss on the cheek and a hug. 'Looks like this platter will feed all three of us – if not more. Drinks have to be ordered over there at the counter and maybe you could get us each another?'

Sabine, mouth full of bread and dip, nodded and gave Sam a thumbs up.

It didn't take Sabine long to realise that Stella's suggestion was the right one. Staying at home and moping would have been a disaster and risked dragging her down into a pit of misery and self-pity. Instead, being in this cosy bar with two livewire friends was a total distraction from herself and her woes. Sam was in fine form – full of chatter about the story he had just completed which dealt with the latest political scandal. It would be the lead story in tomorrow's paper, and he predicted there would be a massive fallout.

'Heads will roll – but if they manage to survive this report – well I have more to follow. My sources are impeccable and trust me completely. I feel like I have just lit a fuse and am now standing back to see how big an explosion it will make – or whether it will spark and cause an enormous wildfire.'

'That's very poetic Sam. You clearly have a way with words. Have you thought about journalism for a career?' teased Stella.

Sam grinned – his face so disarming it was easy to see why his sources would confide in this honest looking man. He turned to Stella.

'Enough about me. You said we were celebrating something tonight. Do tell. What is the cause for celebration?'

Stella waved across at Sabine. 'Madame here was a bit down. Her new romance is blowing hot and cold, and she needed to cheer up – and celebrate something - anything really. Maybe it was just as simple as we now have a great new bar around the corner from our home. And I must say the food and wine so far are excellent. So, let me propose a toast – to our new favourite drinking hole!' Stella raised her glass in the traditional manner of all those proposing a toast.

'Hear, hear,' said Sam as he raised his glass in reply. Sabine followed suit and then proposed a further toast – to good friends – and another toast – to this bar and with increasingly hilarity further toasts followed and were taken up by various people at the adjoining tables.

Drawing breath Sam inquired 'New romance Sabine? Do share. With whom? Tell your Uncle Sam all.' His open and disarming smile invited confidences.

Sabine felt suddenly shy. It was one thing to moan to Stella, but it was quite another to confide in Sam whose good opinion she would like to have. Sabine didn't want to be considered one of those pathetic women who depended on a bloke and yet that was how she was beginning to think she might be becoming. With a smile and a dismissive wave, she sought to channel the strong woman she wanted to be.

'It's nothing. Yes, I am seeing someone, but it's early days. He has a demanding job and it's been hard to coordinate times to meet. He's a barrister and his working hours are all over the place – a bit like those of a journalist I suppose. And Max seems very dedicated...' Sabine's voice trailed off as if she was stuck for excuses for Max's behaviour. Not that it was noticed by Sam who fixated on the mention of Max – a person he knew.

'Max? You mean Max Sumner?' At Sabine's nod he continued. 'You mean that Max coming through the door – over there?'

Stella and Sabine both turned and observed the tall man entering through the front door – waving at the people seated at the bar and heading towards them. A tall red-haired woman appeared to be smiling back at him.

'Max. Over here,' shouted Sam as he waved his arms in the air. Sabine cringed as Stella hissed 'No Sam. Not now.'

'Why not?' Sam was genuinely puzzled.

'Because he pulled out of tonight's arrangements as he was supposed to be working at the office.'

Too late. Max, hearing the shout saw the trio and headed in their direction. The happy smile on his face belied any impression that he had anything to hide.

Arriving at the table and with permission from those at the adjoining table he helped himself to an unoccupied chair – pulling it over he plonked himself between Stella and Sabine all the while smiling happily as if unaware of the hostile gazes from the two women. Sam, never one for delaying clarification and if there was to be a conflict always happy to bring it on asked: 'The girls tell me you were working late. Yet here you are. What a surprise – a lovely surprise no doubt but how come?'

It didn't take much for Max to sense the chill being directed his way by both women. Their silence was a clear indicator given that silence was not the default position for Sabine – that and the lack of expression on both Sabine and Stella's faces. They were waiting to hear his excuse and it was clear it had better be good. There would be no mercy.

'Yes, I was at work,' Max spread his arms out in acceptance of this fact. 'An urgent advice I had to complete. But it ended up being far more straightforward than I expected and took me no time at all. I went to your house Sabine to find you, but all that I could hear was a barking dog when I knocked on the door, so I came searching for you. Thank goodness you are here, or I might have had quite a pub crawl.'

He smiled at his own joke and then as if anticipating Sabine's response continued: 'I did try to call you, but you weren't answering. Maybe it was too noisy for you to hear the phone? Never mind. What can I get you all to drink?'

Was he telling the truth? Sabine wasn't sure. In her mind lingered the vision of Max entering the pub, smiling at that woman and those people by the bar – glamorous strangers to her, but much the same age as them – and Max smiling as if he knew them. Was he really looking for her or were they who he was coming to meet? Clearly Max was not going to explain any further and she felt like it was somehow wrong to suspect that his explanation might not be the truth. Shouldn't she trust Max at his word? One look at his open, happy face as he returned from the bar bearing a tray of drinks was confirmation enough. Her doubting suspicious thoughts must be simply a manifestation of her insecurity. He came looking for her. Shouldn't that be enough?

# Chapter Seventeen

# Sabine the lawyer and a mediation

'Good morning Sabine,' said Rhys as he stopped by her desk. He was clearly in a rush, with a bundle of papers in his arms. 'Now I know you will shortly be moving on to the next rotation in your graduate year and no doubt looking forward to a change, but I thought you might be interested in sitting in on a mediation this week? You recall the matter involving the claim on an estate – our client Gemma McKay?'

At Sabine's nod he continued: 'This Friday the parties are meeting to try and resolve Gemma's claim. Our client told me she was impressed when she met you at our conference and actually asked if you would be there at the mediation. I must say I had not proposed bringing you. I thought Fran and I would be sufficient, but Gemma said something about what she described as your youthful energy giving her strength. Well, whatever works I say – so are you OK to attend? It certainly will be a good experience for you. And an interesting one too, no doubt. We've booked some rooms off site – neutral ground so to speak. My secretary will give you the details and I will make sure you have the necessary papers beforehand. Not that you will be required to say or do anything – apart from looking empathetic and supporting our client with your youthful energy – whatever that means.'

With a wave and a muttered comment about being late for his next meeting he was off leaving Sabine trying to process what had just been said.

Amy who had clearly been listening scooted on her chair around to Sabine's desk.

'What was that about?'

'Not sure. But I think Rhys just cracked a joke' Sabine smiled. 'It looks like I'm about to sit in on my first mediation. He made it very clear that I'm to be a wallflower but still - how weird that the client has requested my attendance at this mediation. It's amazing that she even noticed me last time we met at that conference.'

'Maybe she knew your father?'

'Maybe....'

***

Sabine thought long and hard about what was appropriate attire to wear to a mediation. There was no guidebook as to appropriate attire for such situations. When she asked Stella she was of no help.

'For goodness sake Beanie. Stop fussing. What does it matter? You will be just the baby lawyer in the back corner. Any of your usual black outfits will be fine.'

For some reason that Sabine could not articulate it was important to her that she was at her best for the mediation. Maybe it had something to do with Rhys' comment that their client was looking to her for support. Whatever the reason she selected her outfit with care – a black and white spotted jersey cross over dress that draped like a dream – or so the shop assistant had observed when she tried it on. Sabine also made sure she had thoroughly studied the documents given to her and so on the morning of the mediation she felt not only beautifully presented, but thoroughly prepared.

The same could not be said for their client Gemma, who had arrived early at *Smithtons* in a state bordering on hysteria. Sabine could hear her wailing from Rhys' office.

'Rhys I'm not sure I can do this. You don't understand. My brothers will do anything to get to me and hurt me. It's not about the money to them. They always were jealous. Do I have to be there?' she asked in between choking sobs.

'There. There.' Sabine could hear Rhys speaking in soothing tones. 'Here. Help yourself to a tissue. No. Better still. Have the box and please bring the box with you today. There will be no need for you to see your brothers. You won't be sitting with them. We will be placed in separate rooms and it will always be up to you if you do want to see them. The mediator is there to be the point of contact between both sides. We have a very experienced mediator involved. There's also your barrister, who you've already met and who will look after your interests and if need be, speak to your brothers' barrister on your behalf. Now we must leave shortly. I just have to go and sign something for another matter. Sabine will come and sit with you and maybe get you a water or something hot to drink?'

Sabine, who had been alerted by all the noise was watching from her desk and saw a hand waving frantically in her direction. Clearly her presence was required.

A tear-stained face greeted Sabine as she walked into Rhys' office. Apart from the tears the woman looked so different to last time Sabine had seen her. The wild curly hair now tamed - scraped back into a stylish bun. The long legs encased in fine wool dark check fitted trousers worn with a matching plain sweater. A sombre, yet elegant outfit. Still wearing those massive diamond earrings Sabine noticed, with a hint of envy.

'You remember Sabine Faulkner, don't you?'

A nod and a sniff, then a honk as Gemma robustly blew her nose.

'Sabine will sit with you until it's time to leave. Ah and here is my secretary with a glass of water for you. I won't be long.'

Gemma took a thoughtful sip of her water and then reaching into her cavernous bag withdrew a compact – opened it and surveyed the damage to her make up.

'I look a sight, but I suppose it doesn't matter. Sounds like no-one will see me and certainly no-one will care.'

Sabine knew what response was required.

'No. Not at all. I always think I feel better in myself when my make up is done properly. Like I've got some protection against the world. We've got time if you want to do a quick fix. Not that much really needs doing. Maybe a bit more mascara and just blot around your eyes – see - there where it has run.'

Whatever Sabine had said it seemed to work a treat. With a sniff, Gemma reached into her vast handbag and retrieved a make-up bag and set to work – she had been a model after all, and all that modelling experience now came to the fore as with a few deft touches she repaired the damage then presented her finished face to Sabine for inspection.

'Ta dah,' she said giving a triumphant smile, her recent tears a thing of the past. 'Now we are ready to do battle. Bring it on I say!'

Three adjoining meeting rooms had been booked in a nearby hotel for the purposes of the mediation. Rhys had arranged that they would arrive ten minutes before the others so they would be safely ensconced in their meeting room, thus avoiding any unnecessary interaction and distress for Gemma.

He had already outlined the proceedings before they left *Smithtons*: how the day could be a bit stop/start and that it might take a while for the mediator to establish if there was any common ground or interest sufficient to negotiate a resolution.

'There are some rules to be followed in a mediation and our mediator will make the process very clear at the start. Ah now here is our barrister and Fran.'

The door opened and a tall serious looking woman with spiky dark hair entered closely followed by Fran. The tall lady was a no-nonsense barrister called Erica Rolfe. She sat down next to Gemma and following the usual greetings immediately launched into a discussion about the process to be followed during the day.

'We're lucky to have this mediator today. He is a retired Supreme Court judge with a wealth of experience. I expect he will shortly come in to meet you and may or may not want to speak privately to me and the barrister for the Executors. How the day will pan out will depend much on how he likes to manage things – with our input of course. Our mediator will be wanting to explore what it is we want to achieve today and will be looking for common ground – anything that might point to a way to resolve your claim. This could take some time and if at any time you want to have a break, please let me know.'

Erica had not exaggerated. The whole process did take some time. An entire day in fact. Sabine soon discovered an entire day that lurched from extreme emotion to absolute tedium. With much sitting around. So much handing over of tissues, as Gemma worked through the drama that had been her relationship with her father – and to some extent with her brothers. It soon became clear that the brothers were not prepared to make anything other than a token distribution to their sister who for her part was holding out for a third of the estate.

Still, as their barrister had noted this was progress from the brothers' initial position of giving Gemma nothing from the Estate.

'We can work on this after lunch,' Erica said optimistically after Gemma moaned that it was all *a total waste of time and money.*

'I know this can feel very frustrating as progress is so slow – but there is progress. What would be helpful is if there was something else we could say that might advance your case.' At Gemma's questioning look she elaborated: 'Perhaps something that would give them a reason to justify not only making a distribution but also increasing the amount.'

'Oh, I can give you *something* else,' said Gemma using her hands to signify quotation marks as she said something. 'My brothers are so stuck up – think they are purer than pure and perfect manifestations of the McKay name when the truth couldn't be further off the mark. You see, after mum and dad were told they couldn't have children they adopted two little boys – a baby and a toddler from Victoria – and then surprise, surprise – years later mum fell pregnant and had me. No wonder I was so spoilt. Mum called me her *miracle baby* and of course, dad adored me. Not only his *little gem,* but I was his only biological child. That could be why he was so upset when I went a bit off the rails. He had invested so many of his hopes into me.' Gemma paused, a wistful expression on her face as she contemplated those happy and not so happy times long ago.

'Those adoptions were kept a secret, of course and the world believes those boys are chips off the old man's block – *the next generation nurturing the McKay fortune*, as the media constantly proclaims. Charles and Phillip have played this story to the hilt. They love this mythology of them being true McKays – whatever that means. Now how would it be if the true story got out? That the image they have so carefully nurtured over the years is false, and that in reality they are just cuckoos.'

Erica pondered what had just been said as she thought about how to repackage what Gemma was implying which seemed to be – give me money or I will tell. Perhaps an argument that might work but to an ethical lawyer it did sound a bit too much like blackmail.

'Perhaps what we could say is that as the only biological child of the relationship you should not be penalised and in fact an equal share to each of the adopted children and the only biological child is more than generous – for the adopted children that is.' She thought for a bit longer and with a nod spoke under her breath – 'yes that might work or at least be a good starting point.'

'Well, if you want more – there's heaps.' Gemma was now in full disclosure mode. 'Ours is a family of secrets. Secrets that we have all kept, but if they want to cast me out of the family then there will no longer be any reason to keep stum. My father – hah! He was not the perfect husband and father everyone thinks he was. He had another family you know. Not just a stable of mistresses, but a long-term partner with whom he has one child – now an adult of course. My brothers know about this of course but they like to pretend Della and her boy don't exist. Well, they exist to me and I'm very happy that they are in my life. You've probably seen them photographed with me, but to date we've yet to publicly acknowledge our relationship. Della is a very private person you see.'

Erica held up her hand to halt the flow, as it was clear Gemma was about to launch into further disclosures.

'I think that will do for now. If you don't mind I will have a quick chat with our mediator and see if we can progress your claim. This shouldn't take long.'

And it didn't. With not surprising rapidity the brothers concluded that it was in their best interests to give their sister the third of the estate that she had requested. There was some discussion about which part of the estate should be transferred to Gemma and in the end, she decided that the house in the Southern Highlands and an agreed amount of cash would suit her perfectly.

'I like the idea of a country estate,' she smiled as she spoke. 'Imagine how the neighbours will react to my wild children. That will shake the neighbourhood up a bit. This is more than I need and even better than expected. I am amazed you dragged out of my brothers an undertaking to consult with Della to see if she wants to claim on the estate. I never thought they would acknowledge her role in my father's life.'

Turning to Erica Gemma was effusive in her appreciation. 'Thank you so much. I don't know how you did it but this acknowledgement of my entitlement to a part of the estate means a lot to me. A recognition I suppose that I did count for something.'

'No thanks needed.' Erica brushed off the compliment. 'I think it was of real assistance to our claim that their barrister helped them see it was common sense to settle. Max can be very pragmatic and he would have convinced his clients that no one would benefit from having their family secrets revealed to the public.'

'Max? Max Sumner?' Sabine piped up from where she had been quietly sitting in the corner.

Erica directed her keen gaze at Sabine. 'Yes, that's right. You know him?'

'A little.' Somehow Sabine knew now wasn't the time to disclose how well she knew him.

'He's a very talented barrister and a worthy opponent. Max could go far but I hear rumours that he is being tempted by politics.

Pity.' With that comment any further discussion regarding Max was dismissed as Erica now moved onto consideration of the paperwork needed to record the agreed terms.

It soon became apparent that the mediation was far from over. Considerable time was in Sabine's opinion wasted on the toing and froing involved in drafting and redrafting a deed which outlined all the terms of the settlement of Gemma's claim.

An opinion clearly shared by Gemma who drew a chair up next to Sabine and as they both regarded Gemma's lawyers and barrister in a huddle discussing a contentious clause Gemma settled in for a chat.

'I never knew this process could be so tedious and take so long,' she said.

'Well, at the start this morning I thought it would be over within the hour as it looked like your brothers would not budge. Are you happy with the result?'

'Beyond happy. It kinda hurt that my father cut me out. I know we had our differences, but I thought he still loved me. I'm not sure I will ever forget the deliberate hurt he inflicted by cutting me out of his Will. I guess what I wanted today was the acknowledgement from my brothers that we should be treated as equals. The money was neither here nor there. But don't tell them that! A bit of a shame that I had to disclose family secrets to shame them into doing the right thing. But there you go. Whatever works I say. And once this is over, I will never need to see them again.' She smiled with relief, the tear-stained woman from this morning long gone. No longer tense but bright with anticipation. 'I plan to share dad's house in the Southern Highlands with Della if she wants. My brothers would hate that! She has become a good friend and her son lives down that way.'

Gemma peered intently across at Sabine. 'You look like your father. I can't say I knew your mother, but I certainly met your dad from time to time at functions. Not only do you have his height and colouring but also his sense of being in control. That's why I asked for you to be here today. I rather hoped that might rub off on me and help me get through the day. And it did. Thank you,' she concluded with a smile.

Sometime later – well quite a long time later actually - finalising and signing legal documents seemed to take forever, but eventually after farewelling a very happy and relieved client Rhys, Fran and Sabine headed back to their office.

'What a relief that's over,' said Rhys. 'I was really dreading today. Gemma can be a bit of a challenge but somehow it went smoothly – Erica did a good job I think and Sabine - somehow you seemed to keep Gemma calm. Thank you. You have no idea how easily things can go off the rails with that woman. And she seems to be your number one fan. Watch out you might be about to get your first client.'

Rhys was smiling as he said this. Perhaps he was joking but somehow, she could sense an undercurrent of something else. Sabine knew a lawyer did not give up a client so easily. Was she now a threat to him?

# Chapter Eighteen

# Sabine and Max

Sabine's emotional high lingered for the rest of what remained of her workday and into the evening when she shared her elation with Stella. Her first win – of course she had to share the thrill with her housemate – over and over – until a hurled cushion put paid to the discussion.

'Enough! I'm sick of your silly mediation and your eccentric client. I get that you are very happy with your first experience of a successful outcome and a now grateful client – but please - I have had a long day. My clients are just plain difficult, and I have not had any successes to celebrate. I just want to forget all about the law. Can't we find something mindless on Netflix to watch and eat chips? A true friend would do that.'

More cushions were hurled.

Later on, Sabine's phone rang. It was Max. Should she tell him where she had been today? Would it cause any tension between them having been on different sides of a matter? For a millisecond Sabine pondered this conundrum and then decided to dive right in.

'Hi there. How are things?' She was dying to launch into all her news, but like a well brought up lady Sabine knew how important it was to be interested in the other person's news – even if she wasn't. But then – why wait.

'Guess what? I was at your mediation today. Obviously, you couldn't see me as I was hidden away with our client. It was so interesting. Did you know I was there?'

'Of course not,' came the abrupt reply. 'I was too busy to wonder. But I guess given as Rhys was acting for Gemma McKay your being there should come as no surprise. A good result for your client – she should be happy. In the circumstances for her to get anything from the estate should be considered an excellent result.'

'Mmmm – whatever.' Sabine was inclined not to continue the discussion as it was now obvious they shared different opinions about Gemma. Also, she could see Stella was about to hit play on some enticing drama. 'Were you after something? It's just I have to go.'

A bit of a lie that.

'Nothing much. Just wanted to say hi and see when we could next catch up.' Max could sense that Sabine was distracted and possibly unimpressed by his cool response to her news. Perhaps a treat might tempt Sabine.

'And also, I'm meant to go to a black-tie event this Friday and I was hoping you would join me? It's some type of opening night at the NSW Art Gallery – a private viewing with drinks and nibbles. Interested?'

'The Art Gallery? You mean the latest blockbuster that is opening this weekend? Interested? Too right I am interested!'

Sabine having been brought up by her father to appreciate fine art – (and other fine things – like wine, food etc) and had already heard about this exhibition. A chance to see the paintings without fighting the hordes for sufficient viewing space was something not to be sneezed at. Even more tempting when she considered she would be in the company of this gorgeous, if slightly annoying young man.

Details exchanged she ended the call with a promise to catch up the next day over an early pre-work breakfast.

\*\*\*

'I'm so excited,' said Sabine as she fidgeted in the taxi next to Max. It was Friday evening, and they were on their way to the NSW Art Gallery. Max, looking in Sabine's opinion incredibly handsome in his dinner suit, smiled as he reached around and gave her a hug.

'It's not just the paintings I'm keen to see but just the chance to get dressed up is a treat.'

She smoothed the skirt that had ruched up over her knees. Max was not to know the amount of angst had gone into choosing the right outfit. In the end, after various changes and consultation with an increasingly exasperated Stella, she had decided on a simple black lace dress. The length – just over her knees, with the torso lined in nude fabric but the long sleeves unlined. The sleeves fitted and tapering to a point just above the wrist. The neckline styled in what has been described as a sweetheart neckline displayed her long neck to advantage and hinted at a glimpse of cleavage.

It had taken a while and a fair amount of cursing, but she had managed to fix her hair into a messy bun which she thought enhanced the effect. That and the dangly diamond earrings, a 21st birthday present from her parents – and she was now ready to impress the world.

Upon arrival they were greeted by a stately gentleman just inside the front entrance. Before Max could introduce Sabine, she exclaimed and with arms wide hugged and kissed him.

'Uncle Charles! How wonderful to see you! I didn't know you would be here.'

'My dear Sabine.' Uncle Charles patted her on the back as he returned the hug. 'Of course, I would be here. It is a Liberal Party function after all. You're looking well – and your mother, how is she?' Not giving Sabine time to respond he continued, nodding at Max 'And I see you have come with the fine young man. He is the Liberal Party's face of the future. I have high hopes for him, and we might even find a seat for him in the next election. Max, how are you?' He turned and shook hands with Max. A few more pleasantries were exchanged then with a direction to head inside they moved on leaving Charles to greet the next guests.

'You didn't tell me you knew our Premier?' asked Max as they continued inside. Max was feeling slightly miffed as he had hoped to impress Sabine with his contacts.

'Oh yes. I've known Uncle Charles since I was a child,' said Sabine quite happily unaware of the tension in the young man beside her. 'He and dad were great mates – possibly old school buddies. I'm not certain as they just seemed to have known each other for ages. Not a real uncle of course but that was just what I was expected to call him. Look, over there. It's Aunty Sue. Come on. I'll introduce you.'

As far as Max was concerned the evening went from bad to worse – as Sabine seemed to know everyone in the room. He was introduced to Aunty Sue, the State's Attorney General and then an old school mate who was a recently elected member of the Legislative Assembly. Even those people who lurked in the background of the Liberal Party the so-called power brokers knew Sabine. And while Max could appreciate having a partner such as Sabine with such connections would only help him in his political career, he also felt like he was a lesser person when in the company of this blue blood of society. Not that Sabine noticed. She was too busy having a great time with friends of her fathers to notice how quiet Max was.

'That was such fun,' she said sometime later as they were in yet another taxi heading for Max's apartment at Potts Point. 'So many people there tonight I knew I hadn't seen for ages – well since dad's funeral.'

At that thought her expression became subdued as she remembered her father, the man who had been a friend of all the people she'd met that night and then in her usual way, she shook off her sad thoughts and reverted to happiness. 'Max, thank you so much for taking me. I had such fun. Pity I didn't get to appreciate the paintings. I'll have to find some other time to go there – just for the art and not for the people.'

A thought struck her. 'You didn't forewarn me that it was a Liberal Party do tonight. Was that deliberate?'

'Sort of. I didn't want to put you off. And I wasn't to know you seem you to know all of the Liberal Party. I hope you didn't mind, but I need to network if I'm serious about seeking pre-selection.'

'It's no problem. Dad seemed to know everyone and it probably helped that he went to one of those private schools that churns out our country's leaders. But I suspect if we had gone to a Labour Party function, we also would have had the same result. Sydney can be a small town and Dad just seemed to know everyone. Oh look. We're here already.'

Once inside the front door Sabine grabbed Max by the hand and led him down the corridor with a suggestive twinkle in her eyes.

'Tonight has been such fun.' She said. 'Thank you for inviting me but it just needs a little bit extra to make it perfect. I have something in mind. That is if you don't object?'

That something turned into a lengthy experience that left both of them gasping in delight and more than happy with each other. Sabine quickly fell asleep, but Max lay quietly awake pondering the events of the night. It shouldn't have been a surprise how well connected this woman was. But he had made the assumption that as a young woman having recently entered the workforce, she would be unformed and able to be moulded into the type of person that suited his purposes. Well, he had been wrong there! Max was learning that Sabine was a woman of many parts – beautiful and intelligent of course. But also, more worldly and better connected than he ever thought possible. When he had identified her as the partner who would best further his career Max had thought that with a bit of work, he could bring her along with him. Tonight, however had demonstrated that Sabine could easily become a major asset in his quest for a political career. With her by his side maybe a career in Federal parliament was possible. Gazing at the calm resting face of the young woman gently snoring beside him Max thanked his lucky stars that he had found her.

The next morning, being Saturday meant it was possible to sleep in – for a little while that is – until Sabine remembered Grover.

Abruptly sitting upright in bed, she disturbed Max in his slumbers. The slightly erotic dream that he had been enjoying involving interaction with several demanding women slipped away as Sabine jumped out of bed away from his questing arms.

'Enough of that. I must go. I hadn't realised it was so late. There is a dog to be walked and a brunch to be had. Coming?' Sabine assumed Max would be as interested in this activity as she.

Even half-asleep Max knew not to criticise the precious dog. After all he had been there, done that and had learned his lesson.

A walk in Centennial Park on a sunny Saturday followed by a leisurely brunch made for a very pleasant day which, when merged into an evening spent together, made for perfect happiness. Sabine found herself feeling in total accord with her man. He had been equally attentive to both her and Grover and didn't object when she suggested he stay over at her home – not his.

'You see we have a commitment tomorrow?'

'A commitment?'

'Yes. I think so.' Now she had mentioned it, Sabine wasn't quite sure if she had actually previously told Max. She smiled hopefully.

'We've both been invited to Sunday lunch at Stella's parents' house. I think they want to inspect you to see if you are suitable.'

'Suitable?' Max was genuinely puzzled. Surely Stella's family would have nothing to do with his preselection?

'Suitable for me you duffer! And don't look so scared. You won't be cross examined -well not much. Stella's Nonna is an expert at interrogation but I'm sure you, the experienced barrister will be up for it. Come on you aren't going to chicken out on me, are you? I guarantee an excellent meal of Italian cuisine. You will be safe I assure you. Grover and I will protect you.'

Max threw his hands up in mock surrender. 'OK I give in. Of course, I will go but there's a thought. If Stella's folks are checking me out, when do I get to meet your mother?'

Now that was an excellent question and Sabine acknowledged it as such. It was just – and she wasn't sure how to suggest this – to either her mother or to Max. She was starting to feel like there might be a future with Max. There was so much about him that seemed just right. A few niggles of course – but then who is perfect? Arranging a meeting with her mother? This might be a step too far and had the potential to jinx things. What if her mother looked down her well-bred nose at this man who didn't come from their background? Who even now was rather secretive about his childhood – *You really don't want to know. It was so boring;* he would say when she tried to find out anything about his past and then change the topic or tickle or kiss her. And who seemed to have no relatives – apart from an estranged sister. Any mention of her and he clammed up immediately. Talking about the present and his plans for the future and listening to Sabine natter on seemed to completely occupy their time together and it was only in her solitary moments that Sabine realised how little she knew of Max. Even his so-called friends appeared to be from recent times. She had yet to meet anyone who knew Max before his university days. A mystery perhaps. Or was she over thinking things? Maybe Max just wasn't that interested in where he came from.

Still, it was probably time to introduce him to her mother. And maybe her mother might be able to find out more about this man who was becoming more and more important to her.

'You know what? That's an excellent suggestion. I've been a bit slack and should have done it earlier. There's a good reason to get together – next week in fact. Mum's having a bit of a farewell get together prior to leaving for Melbourne. There will be a few people there – not too many, I hope. It will be our last celebration in the home in which I grew up. So many memories...' Sabine's voice trailed off as she contemplated the range of emotions washing over her as she contemplated saying goodbye to her past. A gentle squeeze of her hand and a solicitous look from Max recalled her to the present. Giving a shake of her head she came back to the present. 'I'm OK. Just feeling a bit sentimental – which comes as a complete surprise I must admit. But it's been the only home I've ever known. Lots of memories – I suppose they will be with me always – but I warn you. I might be a bit teary at mum's farewell party – especially if there are any speeches.'

\*\*\*

Sunday was one of those bright and sunny days that are a delight in Sydney. Not too hot, but warm enough to bask outside without overheating.

'I hope we are sitting outside under the pergola' remarked Sabine as she drove Max to Stella's parents' house. Having been there many times over the years she expertly negotiated back streets until with a triumphant Ta Dah she announced their arrival.

'Looks like Stella has beat us here. Come on inside. Grover and I will protect you if Nonna gets too intrusive.'

The front door had been left open for the expected visitors and Sabine escorted Max through the front gate and down the corridor. This time Stella's father was not in the loungeroom. Grover scampered ahead leading the way towards the delicious smells that were emanating from the back of the house. They entered a kitchen that was a hive of activity. Nonna was busy stirring something bubbling on the stove while Stella's mother Maria, appeared to be fussing over a contraption attached to the table. Meanwhile Stella was nowhere to be seen – although considerable noise and a delicious smell wafting in from outside gave a clue.

Maria looking up as they entered waved them over.

'Sabine just the girl I need. Help me please. This is clearly a two-person job, and that useless Stella has disappeared.'

Catching sight of Max, she exclaimed a greeting.

'Finally, I get to meet Sabine's friend. Welcome – Max, isn't it? My apologies. I can't come over. This stupid sausage machine has got me captive. I don't suppose you two can help?'

'Of course.'

And soon Sabine and Max were deeply involved in the mysteries of sausage making. Pork and fennel flavour – 'Nonna's secret recipe of course,' boasted Maria. 'She should be doing this for I'm sure how I'm doing it will never be quite right for her. But for some reason Nonna has decided to make a tomato sauce to go on the pasta we will cook shortly. Hey Nonna,' she called across the steamy room. 'Look who's here? Our Sabine and her man.'

At the mention of Sabine and her man Nonna's head jerked to attention. Immediately she turned around. Wiping her hands on a stained and faded apron she rushed across – greeted Sabine with kisses on both cheeks and exclamations of delight then turned her full attention to Max. Nonna may have been a very small lady of advanced age, but the intensity of her regard made Max squirm with embarrassment. Her gaze had all the intent of an experienced interrogator – anticipating the secrets she planned to extract from him.

Then to his relief she smiled, pinched his forearm and exclaimed. 'What a handsome man and so tall. Sabine, you have done well. He's a lawyer, is he?'

'Mama please,' protested Maria. 'Leave the poor man alone. He's only just arrived. Let him relax. Back to your cooking. Shouldn't the pasta go on now. Leave Max to help me make the sausages. There will be plenty of time for you to grill him over lunch.'

With a sigh of relief Max turned to help Maria manipulate the sausage machine and to hope that come lunch he would be sitting far away from Nonna.

And he was. Not that this helped him avoid any cross examination. Everyone, including the young children was curious about him and seemed intent on knowing more about Sabine's new *special friend*.

It was an exhausting afternoon for Max and took all of his concentration to ensure that he stuck to his publicly known life story and that he didn't let anything else slip. Mind you, he thought, he now had sympathy for those criminals who were grilled by the police. It would be so easy to divulge something else and then there was the terrifying thought that Stella's Nonna would pounce and that would be the end of things. But somehow, he came through the afternoon's grilling unscathed. Drawing on his charm and whenever the questioning delved too deeply into Max's background, he was able to divert the interrogator by asking questions of his own. Sabine was no help. She seemed quite entertained by the ordeal. Something he said to her on the way home.

'You were no help when Nonna and Maria were at me. Couldn't you have intervened?'

'No way.' Sabine took her attention off the road and gave Max a laughing glance. 'Now you know what I've had to suffer whenever I visit. They have no mercy those women. And I'm sure Stella was grateful you were the focus of their attention today. Besides it was rather entertaining seeing you squirm.'

'Entertaining? Humph.' Max was not impressed. Making a mental note to never again venture out to one of those Sunday lunches he crossed his arms, stared straight ahead and lapsed into a brooding silence.

It had been said by others that Sabine was not the most observant of people. Yet on the return trip even she could sense that Max was experiencing what she was coming to refer to as *a bit of a mood*. Best to be ignored until he came good.

'Will I drop you off at your place? No doubt you have work to do?'

The grunt he gave she took for assent. The late afternoon Sunday traffic was surprisingly civilised and it didn't take long to reach Potts Point. A quick peck on the cheek and a *I'll ring you later*, then Max was out of the car and headed for the apartment block entrance without a backward glance and only a desultory wave of his hand.

'Well Grover that wasn't what I expected,' said Sabine. An exhausted Grover was lying sprawled on the back seat. Hearing his name looked up and waited expectantly for his mistress to continue.

'I had a good time, but clearly Max did not. Maybe it was all a bit much That large, noisy family and all those questions. He seemed reluctant to talk much about his background. I wonder why? Maybe a family tragedy or some other trauma lurks in the background? I wonder?'

Grover was not wondering at all. Humans were a mystery to him. He saw no need to think too deeply about them so long as he was fed and walked. But he could sense his favourite human was concerned. Perhaps a helpful whine might make her feel her concern was shared?

No. It didn't. But as a distraction it helped.

'Oh Grover. I suppose you are right. A walk is what we need to do. Too much sitting around all afternoon makes for overthinking things. When we get home, we will go for a long walk straight away. If nothing else, we both need to walk off lunch. I saw how much food the girls were slipping you under the table. No dinner for you tonight.'

Having said this Sabine knew it was a threat often made, but rarely followed through.

The rest of the day passed quickly. A walk with Grover, a debrief on the day's events with Stella who was equally puzzled about Max's mood and a quick call to Anna to sort out arrangements for emptying of the family home.

'There is still quite a bit of your stuff here Sabine which you will need to sort. Soon I hope, as I have to vacate the house within the month. I will put a lot of the furniture in storage until I work out where I will settle permanently. Some of the other stuff – assuming you don't want any of it? – well I suppose I will sell what I can and give the rest to charity. Is that OK with you?'

'Of course. We have enough here – except maybe one or two of those comfy chairs in the loungeroom and a painting or two if you can spare them. Would it suit you if I pop in during the week after work to sort out what I can have?'

Arrangements made and agreed Sabine hung up and contemplated what to do with the rest of the evening. Clearly whatever she was going to do would not involve Max. She sensed that somehow, she would not be hearing from him tonight. For her part she wasn't too keen on speaking to a grumpy man. It wasn't her fault that he found today hard going. Maybe a quick message texted to him thanking him for coming with her to lunch and suggesting a catch up during the week would be enough.

***

Max meanwhile had other matters to concern himself with, and perhaps it was the thought of these imminent obligations that was also contributing to his grumpy mood. After Sabine deposited him at his apartment building at Potts Point, he headed not to his apartment but instead caught the lift down a floor straight to his basement car parking space and drove out of the building. Max's car like everything else in his life was sleek, expensive yet understated. A silver sedan, being a recent model of European design. Not too showy but not too cheap either. He sped out the motorway heading west – further out than where they had been today and after half an hour he arrived at his destination.

Max slowed as he turned into the street he hadn't visited for years. The houses were still shabby and unloved. The gardens untended and half dead and the cars on the nature strip equally shabby. Taking care to avoid an overturned garbage bin he pulled into the driveway of what must be the worst house in the street. Nothing had changed since he had lived here and seeing it today made his surly mood even worse. He should be glad he had left all this behind, yet somehow today of all days confronting the reality of his past made him wish he had not returned. But when his mother had rung she had made it clear that staying away was not an option.

The screen door opened and there she stood. Smaller than when he last saw her which if he was honest with himself was years ago – and greyer.

'So, you came then?'

Not a hello or a loving hug.

Nor a hug from Max.

'I'm here because you told me to. You said it was important. Well, here I am. What is it you want? I haven't got long.'

His mother sighed. Holding the screen door open she stood aside and beckoned him in then gestured that he should turn right into the lounge room. This room was largely unchanged since Max's childhood - furnished with a shabby three-seater brown vinyl lounge, an electric heater in a chimney alcove and in the far corner a dining room table – clearly not used for eating, judging by the piles of papers and magazines scattered over the top. The large screen TV that dominated the room made it clear what was the real focus of this room.

Max sat carefully on the lounge after having dusted some food crumbs away – evidence of meals that had been eaten while seated on the lounge and watching TV.

Christine sat in the matching armchair and cleared her throat and then in some agitation launched into the reason for their meeting.

'I know you are busy and – well - have moved on from all this – but I thought you needed to know …' her voice trailed off as with deep concentration Max's mother looked down and studied her twisting hands.

'Well, what?' Max spoke harshly. He didn't have time for all this. She had dragged him out here to struggle town – the last place he ever wanted to see again – and now she was taking forever to get to the point. He just needed to sort out whatever was bugging his mother and get the hell out of here. Did she need money? Judging by the state of the place maybe that was the problem. Well, that was one problem he could easily sort out.

'Do you need money? Is that the issue? Tell me how much and I'll sort out a transfer.'

Christine shook her head.

'No son. It isn't that. Although being on the pension money is always tight. I need to tell you that I'm … '

She paused and then spoke in a rush as if getting the words out in a hurry would make them less than real and negate their impact. 'It's just that I'm not well. I'd been feeling a bit off colour and went for a check-up the other week – I had a few tests – that sort of thing you know?'

Again, another pause, as if Christine could not bring herself to say the fatal words – although Max was starting to suspect that he could already guess what she was about to say.

'The doctor tells me it's cancer. Apparently, it is everywhere, and I haven't got long to go. In a way it is a relief as I won't need to struggle through the ordeal by chemo with all that pain and little prospect of success.'

'Cancer?' Max was at a loss as to how to react. Was he meant to encourage his mother to hope for a cure? Or give her comfort? Neither option was very appealing to him. It was hard to remember a time when they had been close, but she was his mother, so he supposed he had to say something. They were sitting too far apart for him to reach out and in any event hugging or touching his mother was not an instinctive response.

'What do you want me to do?'

'You're a lawyer. I want you to draft my will. What little I have I want to go to my grandchildren – Leanne's children.' With a dismissive glance at Max, Christine continued: 'You need nothing, and Leanne is now settled, so I would like my jewellery and possessions to go to the kids – or they can sell them if they wish. This house belongs to the government – there is really only my car and a few things. It won't take you long to prepare a will. I will be moving to the hospice in the next day or so – maybe even tomorrow. Leanne will take me. And you can bring the will there for me to sign. As I said I don't have long to go.'

Having said her piece Christine rose and headed for the front door. It was clear that the discussion was over, and he was expected to leave. The hesitancy with which she moved gave clue to the pain she was feeling – that and the tightness about her lips. Not that Max noticed. However, he was aware he was being dismissed and was more than happy to leave. All he wanted was to be out of this appalling place. A quick peck on his mother's cheek and a squeeze of her arm and he was gone – returning to his eastern suburbs stamping grounds as quickly as possible. Once home Max poured himself a very large glass of red wine, wandered out onto the balcony and ignoring the distant harbour vista, proceeded to analyse the situation. He was a lawyer after all and thinking objectively came easily to him.

His mother was dying. Awful for her and possibly for Leanne. Although maybe not, for he hadn't seen Leanne for years. Maybe she was as absent in his mother's life as he was. Yet there was mention of grandchildren. How many? Possibly more than one as his mother spoke of them in the plural. Not that he knew exactly, for why would Leanne tell him when they no longer spoke? But his mother must have been in contact with them.

Max dredged deep into his very being to consider his response to the news about his mother's imminent death. And while he felt some pity about her suffering, his reaction seemed to him to be no more than if he had heard that an acquaintance had died. His mother was so removed from his life that any impact from her passing would be less than the slightest ripple in a pond. Max rubbed his eyes. It had been a long day after all and he was feeling exhausted. The lunch and trying not to be tricked out by all those useless questions from those annoying people had tested his resolve. Did he really want to persist with Sabine, lovely though she was, when she had such annoying prying friends? He was convinced they were just seeking to trip him up. Sabine was so open and trusting and took on face value everything he told her. Not her friend Stella. Max suspected she was suspicious of him although she had yet to say anything overtly hostile.

And what about his mother? He supposed he needed to visit her at the hospice. Appearances were important and it would look bad if he wasn't seen to care. But then what should he tell Sabine?

Should he tell her anything? Max tried to remember if he had told her his mother was dead or had he said they were estranged? His usual approach when the question of family was raised in conversation was to look sad and say something like *It's all too complicated. Let's not go there.* He would then smile sweetly and look away. Nearly every time when saying something like that, it had been enough to close down the discussion.

Thinking back to all their contact, Max decided it was probably safer to say something. After all he should contact Sabine to thank her for today. He suspected she would be waiting to hear from him.

And she was.

'I thought I would have heard from Max by now,' she complained to Stella. 'I know he said something about work to do but I would have thought he would be done. It's after 9,'

Sabine's brow wrinkled in concern. She didn't want to divulge to Stella how sulky Max had been, but it was possible Stella had sensed this.

'Maybe he has a case of too much Nonna. She can be a bit overpowering if you are not prepared! Although I think Nonna and Mum approved of Max. Well to be honest any single man of marriageable age would meet their approval!'

As if on cue Sabine's phone pinged. It was a message from Max. It read:

*Sorry it's a bit late I know. Thanks for today. I really enjoyed being invited. It's been a bad afternoon and I thought I should let you know I may be a bit hard to contact in coming weeks. I've had bad news tonight. My mother is ill and it is terminal. I'll talk tomorrow. It's a bit much to take in.*

Sabine's immediate reaction was of horror. She handed her phone to Stella who silently read the message.

'Oh no. Poor Max. Should I call him?'

'It sounds like he wants to be on his own. But you know what? If this was my mother, I would want you to call. So why don't you call and if he doesn't want to talk, he will let it go to Message Bank.

Max answered on the first ring. Sabine rushed to speak before Max could say anything.

'I had to ring to check how you are. Max I'm so sorry. What terrible news. Are you OK?'

Max was silent as if he was struggling to find the right words. He was – but not in the way Sabine was thinking. It wasn't that he was choked with grief as Sabine would expect. It was more that he was trying to work out what to say that would ensure the best response.

'I'm sorry. It's been all too much.' He spoke quietly. Max thought: well, that is true but probably not the way Sabine would expect. 'I've had a shocker of a day. Mum is seriously ill and it came as a big surprise.' No lie there either.

As he expected Sabine took his words at face value. Having recently experienced the loss of a parent her first thoughts were of empathy and compassion. She didn't question why this was the first time she had heard of the existence of Max's mother.

'You poor dear. Can I do anything? Would it help if you came over here for the night? Maybe being with us might ease the pain?'

Yes, it might. Perhaps it was the thought of death, but all he wanted to do was be with Sabine. To be really close with Sabine. To absorb her energy in the most primal way – sex – yes that's what he needed. Lots of it. That way he would be able to sleep and blot out all of the day's events.

'You might be right. It's a bit gruesome being here on my own. I'll come over to you – that is if you and Stella can bear having me at your place tonight? I promise, I will try not to be too morose.'

'It's no problem. Stella's gone to bed anyway,' she said shooing a bemused Stella away. 'I'll make some hot chocolate and I'll be waiting for you. See you soon.'

# Chapter Nineteen

## Sabine the young lawyer

Monday started in a rush. They had been late to bed what with one thing and another, and both Max and Sabine had slept in. If it hadn't been for Grover nudging his mistress because of his urgent need to get outside they would have slept in much longer.

'Oh shit,' exclaimed Sabine glancing at her watch and seeing the time. 'I'm going to be so late and this is the one day I must be on time. Shit, shit, shit. Grover no walk for you. I'll let you outside and leave the back door open while I have a shower.' She shoved Max who was still sound asleep, on his back with his mouth wide open. Not a pretty sight but Sabine in her panic did not notice. 'Max, do wake up! We're so late. I've got my performance review at 9.30 and I have to rush.'

She could hear her voice rising as the panic set in.

Max opened one sleepy eye, assessed the situation then rolled over and spoke calmly as if speaking to a toddler:

'Don't panic. Get dressed and I'll drive you to work. I've got the day off to sort out mum. I can walk Grover if you wish after I've dropped you off at work and I'll bring him back here before I go out to see her. See – it will all be fine. Just go get ready.'

A quick hug and with an enthusiastic *you really are a life saver*, Sabine bolted out from the room towards the bathroom.

She was deposited outside her work with minutes to spare before she was due to see Rhys and Fran. Amy had already turned on her computer and left a notepad open on Sabine's desk to make it look like she was already there. A steaming cup of coffee was also in place.

'Amy, you are a wonder. I truly owe you one – or two, or more. And thanks so much for the coffee,' said Sabine gratefully sipping on the coffee.

'I was beginning to wonder if you would turn up today. I didn't know if I should ring you. Luckily for you Rhys and Fran are also running late. I heard his assistant taking a call from him – something to do with the traffic. So now you have a little while to settle. My review is later this morning. It looks like you are the first on today. Lucky you. No time for nerves that way.' Amy smiled reassuringly as Sabine grimaced.

'Oh no. Here they come. Wish me luck,' said Sabine taking one last gulp of her coffee before turning and heading towards the beckoning Rhys who was standing by the doorway to his office.

'Good morning Sabine,' he grinned, slicked back still damp hair and a relaxed outdoorsy glow to his face made it clear why he was late that morning. Sabine could only surmise that the waves must have been breaking, but she was not brave enough to ask.

Inside Fran was already seated at a small round table, papers spread out before her. A colourful scarf once again draped twice around her neck and tied in an intricate arrangement. Sabine smiled a welcome and tried not to stare too closely. Yes, the scarf was tied in such a way that her neck was fully covered, and Fran was looking pale, but then wasn't she always looking pale these days? Maybe she should find time to check in with Fran? But not now. It was time to focus on being the best graduate lawyer ever. Sabine straightened her spine and with a confident smile she channelled her mother's elegant stance as she moved across and sat down at the table.

Rhys cleared his throat, gazed down at some handwritten notes scrawled on a pad before him launched into the review.

'Sabine. It's been three months since you joined our team, and I must say it has been a very interesting time having you with us.'

*Interesting?* This didn't sound like praise to Sabine. She tried not to tense and focussed on keeping a polite smile pasted onto her face.

'You came to us with such an outstanding academic record, yet during the first few weeks, we both could sense you were struggling. It may have been because of your recent bereavement, and the firm certainly made some allowances for that.'

*Allowances?* Sabine steeled herself. This could only be said to foreshadow bad news. Were they going to sack her?

Rhys smiled. 'Yet after what I'm sure you will agree was a shaky start you have really come into your own. Fran and I couldn't be happier with your performance. Both your legal skills and your written advice work are beyond what we expect from a junior lawyer. Researching and finding that relevant case to include in that recent advice was most impressive. Furthermore, your people skills are excellent as demonstrated by your ability to engage with clients in the way you did with Gemma. Gemma is still singing your praises. In fact, she commended you to our managing partner and he now wants you on his team. Well done, but I hope when the time comes for you to nominate your permanent placement you select our team. Isn't that right Fran?'

Fran nodded in response, then went on to add her bit.

'Sabine. I know your next placement will be with the Media team, and I'm sure that will be most interesting for you. But I hope you won't forget us here in Dispute Resolution. I am always here to help or be a sounding board if you need a second opinion.' Fran's goodwill was obvious by the warmth of her friendly smile.

All in all the performance review went well as Sabine later outlined to an anxious Amy.

'They were so kind. Even the negative comments were nicely framed. Thank goodness that's over. I felt like I was back at school getting a bad report. You must be soon?'

'Next I think.'

Wishing her good luck which she was sure Amy didn't need, she was such a swat after all, Sabine turned to head back to her desk and as she did she noticed Fran returning to her office. There was no time to waste. Time to get Fran on her own.

As she knocked on the door of Fran's office Sabine observed her standing pensively looking out the window. At the sound of the knock, she turned.

'Have you a moment?'

'Of course. Come in Sabine,' she smiled and gestured to the chair.

'I just wanted to say how much I have appreciated your kindness and help in the last few months. It's been a bit of a shock coming to a workplace after uni and you have really helped make the transition so much easier. In a way I'm sorry to be moving on although I appreciate my desk will only be just down the corridor.'

Fran brushed off Sabine's thanks. 'You are most welcome and no need to thank us. It has been a pleasure to have you here with us. I just hope you seriously consider returning to our team at the end of your graduate stint.'

'I'm certainly tempted, and ...' Sabine drew breath as she wondered how to tactfully address her concerns. Then in her typical style she dived right in – 'I'm hoping that you will call on me if you still need me in any way. I sometimes wonder how you manage to juggle this amazing workload with being a mum and no doubt a sleep deprived mum. So, if I can help in any way, please call on me. I'm happy to do a bit of extra research or if it is time out at home you need, I am always happy to babysit while you have a break. My spare time is my own – well apart from the demands of a little dog and an occasional boyfriend.'

Sabine smiled in what she hoped was an encouraging manner. She could see that Fran had not expected her to say this and by her delayed response she wondered if Fran was at a loss for words. Then with a serious expression she responded.

'Thank you, Sabine. Thank you for caring. You have no idea how much what you have said means to me.' At this her eyes became glassy with unshed tears. Giving an unladylike sniff Fran continued: 'Yes, it has been a challenge. All the reading and preparation in the world has not prepared me for how hard it is to be a working mum – especially being the mother of a child that doesn't sleep. I'm told that will pass but will I still have my sanity by the time it does?' A weak smile accompanied this feeble attempt at humour.

'That does it. I'm definitely up for babysitting – that is if you trust me? I could take young Mia for a walk while you nap – anytime on the weekend? Deal?'

'Deal. The thought of a nap is so tempting. Let's plan to do something this weekend if it suits. Here's a card with my mobile number on it and if you would text me yours, we can make plans. Now I must go back to Rhys' office for another performance review. Sabine, I think you have just made my day.' And with a smile and a quick hug Fran left the office and headed down the corridor, a discernible bounce to her step.

*Well that's a good start* thought Sabine. With a bit of luck she might be able to sort out Fran's problems or at least give her the courage to deal with it on her own. In any event she quite liked Fran and the thought of a new friend was always appealing – plus the lure of a baby. A baby she could play with, but hand back when it became too much. Perfect!

The rest of the morning passed quickly. It didn't take long to pack up her belongings and move them on a trolley to a new cubicle further down the corridor on the western side of the building. She would have to remember to turn left out of the lift in future. The new area had the same generic blandness of her previous workspace. Partners' and Associates' offices lined the external walls of the building, each with a large picture window that looked out onto a cityscape and glimpses of distant views. Her cubicle was one of many occupying the internal area. To her surprise Amy was once again her neighbour.

'I thought you were going to Mergers and Acquisitions?'

'So did I.' Amy shrugged. 'But apparently there was a sudden change of plan so here I am. And to be honest I would rather stay with you. Being part of the Media team certainly sounds exciting, but also rather terrifying. It will be much better having you around.'

Personally, Sabine thought Amy's confidence in Sabine's abilities was misplaced. As far as she was concerned they were equally in the dark. From what she had heard the Media team was a pressured environment. She understood they acted for a stable of high-profile clients: national newspapers and TV stations, various celebrities and the occasional politician in their defamation and contempt proceedings. It certainly sounded like the work could be interesting, but Sabine suspected that like their last placement any contact with such important clients would be extremely limited.

That afternoon they met the practice team at a meeting which started as a work planning meeting and ended as a social occasion over afternoon tea. The new team was quite a contrast to what they had just left behind. An older senior partner called William Clarke was in charge. By Sabine's estimation he appeared to be a man in his fifties or maybe even older – a bit no nonsense and with that sort of private school accent just like that of her father. With distinctive features featuring a square cut jaw, a beaky nose and sleekly styled steel grey hair he was someone she recalled from the interviewing committee when she applied to be accepted in the graduate program. She remembered he was the committee member who was no-nonsense and asked the tricky questions.

William was so different to the easy-going, casually attired Rhys. It was hard to imagine they were partners in the same firm – she couldn't imagine they would have any hobbies or interests in common. The thought of William discussing perfect breaks like Rhys did on a regular basis made her smile. As did the thought of anyone calling him Willy or Bill.

Even his introduction to her and Amy was so different to the casual greeting Rhys had given them on their first day.

'Welcome Amy and Sabine to the Media team. I like to think of us as the lead lawyers at *Smithtons*' William said as he waved the two women to their seats around a large table in the meeting room tucked away at the corner of the building. Four other people were already seated: two Sabine recognised as paralegals whose work crossed over various legal teams and two others who were strangers to her.

'Let me introduce you to the team. This is Penny Nesbitt our Senior Associate.' He waved at a young woman seated across the table – red shaggy cropped hair and attired in a navy-blue suit. She smiled a greeting at the two women. And next to Penny is Mei Clarkson who has recently been promoted to Associate- a well-deserved promotion I might add.' A dainty woman of Asian appearance waved her greeting. 'And these are our two hard working paralegals. Charles and Anita whom I believe you may already have met?

Greetings exchanged William settled into chairing the meeting with the decisive manner of one who was always in command.

'Amy and Sabine, I can guarantee you will be very busy during your time with us. I expect you chose media as your second placement to extend any knowledge you acquired at university and I can assure you that you won't be disappointed. We have very demanding clients – publishers of major broadsheets and magazines, one TV network for starters and a few high-profile people whom we look after on occasion. Our clients expect us to be available at all times, so you may find that you will be expected to be on call – once you are up to speed with the subject matter that is. To start with – maybe this week and next I expect you will be shadowing Mei or Penny. They will be your supervisors and your immediate contacts.'

Introductions over William now referred to a printout and started to review with the others progress on various matters while Amy and Sabine sat silent. As Amy confessed later she had not studied Media Law at university and everything that had been said was a mystery to her. 'Me too,' confessed Sabine.

They had both listened intently as the discussion swirled around them concerning the expected response to the issue of a *Concerns Notice* late the previous week. Although no formal response had been received Penny indicated she expected the recipient would address their client's concerns.

Noticing Sabine's puzzled expression Penny elaborated.

'It's part of the process. We are required to issue a *Concerns Notice* before starting litigation as a way of giving the person who made or published the defamatory comment an opportunity make amends. In this case I think it will get sorted as it is a rather straightforward matter– being just a situation of a sportsman flying off the handle and making some very nasty allegations about a competitor in the heat of the moment. I'm sure once this individual has calmed down and got a bit of legal advice he will issue the apology our client requires.'

'Moving on,' said William with a quick downwards glance at his watch:' where are we up to with the *Daily News* case Mei?'

'We have a hearing date and a conference with Counsel later this week. A fair bit of work to be done – Amy and Sabine - one of you will be helping me with this. Penny and I will sort out who will be doing what, and let you know.'

The discussion turned to a number of other matters. By now Sabine's head was spinning. She was trying to take some notes, but nothing seemed to make sense. Again, that feeling of being out of her depth. The conversation turned to who would be on call this week. On call? Like they were doctors at a hospital?

'I'll take this week,' said Penny. I have nothing planned, so I can take the phone now if you like William.'

William passed over a mobile phone which Sabine later learned was closely guarded by the lawyers. This was affectionately known as the *bat phone* and was the point of contact at any hour of the day for their major publishing and broadcasting client. Sabine was later to dread hearing that phone ring as she never knew what the caller would be seeking her opinion about. Sometimes the questions would be straightforward and what was contained in the draft newspaper article or tv script was so obviously defamatory that she wondered why they had bothered calling. Other times, when matters were way beyond her experience, she had to take notes and consult Penny or Mei. Those occasions were frankly quite terrifying.

Later that evening Sabine was feeling a bit more positive as she mentally reviewed the day. Her positive performance review showed she could be a good lawyer and she told herself she should feel confident about taking on new challenges. Her thoughts turned to Max and what he was going through. After all anything that had happened in her day must be better than looking after a dying mother. As Sabine's thoughts turned to Max as if on command her phone rang. It came as no surprise to her then that the caller was Max inquiring about her day.

'It all a bit strange,' she said in response to Max's question. 'But the work sounds like it might be interesting. It's just I don't know anything about defamation law. I suppose I need to read a few cases – do a bit of homework as they all seem to assume Amy and I studied Media Law at uni. I mean - how hard can it be? Anyway, enough about me – what is happening with you and how is your mother?'

'Ah you don't want to go there,' Max automatically gave his standard response and then realised that for once this would not satisfy Sabine. In these circumstances she would want to know more.

That morning Christine had been moved by ambulance to the hospice which was located not far from his mother's home. Max omitted to mention that he had not been present when this occurred. Instead, he had been at his chambers catching up on some advice work. It was only in the afternoon following a call from the hospice that he drove there with a draft will for his mother to sign. The hospice was a modern, purpose-built sprawling one storey building with rooms looking onto restful gardens. The décor and the manner of the staff was welcoming in a peaceful way. Leanne, Max's sister was already there – seated by the side of the bed holding her mother's hand. She looked up as the door opened, her eyes widening in surprise as she recognised the little brother who she had last seen many years ago.

'Oh, it's you. No point your being here. Mum's asleep.'

'No, I'm not,' came a quavering voice from the bed as Christine struggled to sit upright.

'Here let me help you.' Leanne solicitously hovered propping her mother up with several cushions and carefully wrapping a shawl around her bony shoulders.

'Don't fuss,' Christine mumbled as she batted Leanne's hands away. Her attention was on her son. 'Did you bring it?'

'Yes. I've got it here. Please read it and check for accuracy and I will then locate a couple of nurses to be the witnesses. If you're happy with it and you need no further alterations, you can sign it tonight.'

'Sign what?' Leanne was suspicious.

'Mum's will. She asked me to draw it up.'

'Typical! We never see you but now mum is dying you are here to scavenge what you can. Have you no shame!' Leanne's voice quivered with emotion as she scrabbled in her bag for a tissue.

'Here, take the box,' said Max as he handed her the box of tissues that were on the bedside table. 'You've got it all wrong. Once again, you've jumped to conclusions. I'm here to help.'

A disbelieving snort greeted Max words. The arrival of the doctor put an end to the siblings' sparing. The doctor took Max by the arm and led him outside the room.

'Your mother is fading fast. Her organs are failing, as her body shuts down. It's most likely that she doesn't have long. We have increased her pain relief, but I expect she will not linger for more than a day or so. I'm sorry but the least we can do is make her comfortable. I'll leave it to you to update your sister. I'm sorry' he repeated and then moved away on to the delivery of more sad news to the next family.

'So that is where we are up to;' said Max as he concluded his update to Sabine. 'I'm staying here tonight. Leanne has gone home to her children.' It was an indication of how stressed Max really felt as in an unguarded moment he let slip 'and to be honest I'm quite glad she's not here. She has been making it all so difficult with her dramatics.'

'Dramatics?'

Max realising this was not the most sympathetic observation and tried to remedy the situation.

'I mean she is very emotional and understandably so, but it is the last thing Mum needs. She just needs to be not stressed and be at peace. The chaplain is coming around shortly and that might give her some comfort. I'd better go. I can see she is looking restless. I'll ring tomorrow.'

The next morning when Max rang, it was to report that his mother had passed away at first light.'

'It was weird. As the night progressed her breathing became more and more laboured. I now know what they mean by a death rattle. The time between each breath became longer and I was starting to expect there not to be another breath, but then there was. And then at first light she stirred. Her eyes opened and she said *Charlie* in the happiest voice. Which is weird as she never had anything nice to say about my long-gone father. And then – with a sigh like a deflating tyre – the softest of sounds – she just exhaled and was dead.'

Max fell silent as he contemplated the passing of his mother – this woman who should have figured large in his life but hadn't. He supposed he was meant to feel sad, but all he felt was an absence of emotion. Nothing. But he knew this was not something he could share with Sabine as it would be beyond her understanding or life experience.

'I'm so sorry Max. What can I do? Do you want me there? You shouldn't be alone.'

'Sabine I'll manage. There's a bit to sort out here and I'm waiting for Leanne to arrive so we can speak to the funeral director. All a bit gruesome I know, but it has to be done and mum left specific instructions that we will have to follow although I suspect Leanne will not want to. There's to be no funeral – only a private cremation. I expect I will be in for a bit of a scene from Leanne when she finds this out. Not something to look forward to. If I could see you tonight that would – I don't know – give me something to look forward to perhaps?'

Sabine could sense she was missing something. Max seemed so – so stoic? Maybe he was in shock? The least she could do was be a good friend and comfort him tonight.

'Of course. I will be there waiting for you – always.'

Always? As soon as the words were out of her mouth she shuddered. Did she really mean that? But it was too late to take the words back and judging from Max's grateful reaction she was now stuck – unable to say anything further or to take it back.

# Chapter Twenty

# Farewells

Christine's farewell was exactly as she had lived her life – a non-event. Sabine was surprised to discover that not even Christine's children had attended her cremation. Max had explained that this was in accordance with his mother's wishes. The cleaning out of her home and disposal of her possessions had been done by Leanne. What pitiful assets she had – a small balance in her savings account and some gold jewellery - were shared amongst her two grandchildren. And that was that.

Max reverted to being the Max she knew – kind, solicitous and happy to discuss his work and hers but unless questioned, made no further mention of his mother or his sister. It was as if the door had closed on that chapter of his life. When Sabine, not able to help herself did ask something about his mum or wondered how his sister was coping it was as if a wall immediately went up as Max in his polite way made it very clear that such questions were out of order. Sabine, puzzled about how a person could behave in this manner, she shared her concerns one evening when she rang her mother.

'Sabine, not everyone is an open book like you. Maybe Max is a very private person and keeps much to himself. Let him be and don't nag. If he wants to share his feelings about his bereavement he will. Give him space.'

'I do! All he now wants to talk about is his upcoming pre-selection. I thought he had it in the bag but apparently some other contender has come out of left field. I would have thought so close to his mother's death he might be a bit more subdued, but he seems all fired up to win.'

'It could be he is using it as a distraction to take his thoughts away from his mother. Just be there for him my dear. And bring Max to my farewell party. It's on Saturday night next weekend. So don't forget to come and say goodbye to the house. By Monday everything will be packed up and put into storage. Don't let me have to remind you again – this is your last chance to take anything you want.'

'Ma!' Sabine's voice rose in panic. She was not ready to farewell the family home – and her mother. Surely her mother should be less no-nonsense and a bit more emotional about saying goodbye to what had been a large part of her life? But all she could sense were the waves of excitement emanating from Anna. As if she couldn't wait to be off on her new adventure.

By Saturday Sabine was exhausted. Each evening she had been studying defamation, copyright and contempt case law in an effort to understand what was being discussed every day at work. Despite all this hard work she still felt ignorant and left in the dark. Amy was no help. She was just as lost as Sabine. One advantage however was that when she was asked to prepare some dot points on the most recent Federal Court decision – an appeal from a controversial single judge decision, she was able to churn it out at quick speed having read the decision the night before.

Neither Amy nor Sabine had been asked to mind the *bat phone,* but they knew it was only a matter of time. This imminent threat hung over their heads like a Sword of Damocles. It was a fate they knew they could not avoid. It didn't help that Penny assured them the phone rarely rang. Sabine didn't believe her.

Halfway through the week Fran had checked in to see how Amy and Sabine were coping with the transition to a new team. Over coffee they both shared their anxieties with her.

'It's all so strange and new,' said Amy 'But I'm sure we will get the hang of it in no time,' she said, ever the optimist.

'Hang in there. You are both very smart and hardworking and if they don't appreciate you, just remember Rhys and I want you both back. William is actually a very good lawyer and you could learn a lot from him. Just don't be put off by his manner. He can be a bit abrupt – grumpy even. And be warned. He's one from the old school. He believes in the hierarchy of lawyers. Now that William has met you he will not expect to have anything further to do with baby lawyers like you unless you are in the company of the Associates. No open-door policy there! Penny and Mei are really the people you must interact with. You will be fine I'm sure but please remember if you have any concerns, feel free to come and chat with me - anytime.'

'Now I'm really worried,' Sabine confided in Amy later on when they were heading back to their desks. 'Reading between the lines it sounds like William is a grumpy old sod who is stuck in the dark ages when all lawyers were male. And why would Fran offer to be there for us if she wasn't worried about how we would be treated?'

Amy shrugged. There was nothing more to be said. They were both in uncharted territory, but at least they had each other.

***

It had taken Sabine much thought and preparation to achieve the result that she was now inspecting in the full-length mirror in her bedroom. She had wanted to make an effort for her mother. This farewell party was a big thing in Anna's life and the least she could do was to make an effort with her appearance. Sabine had styled her hair with so much product that it shone a glossy gold. Painstakingly styled into softly falling curls that fell around her face and to her shoulders it looked gorgeous – or so she thought.

Sabine didn't want to disappoint her mother on this special night and had put a lot of thought into the selection of an outfit that would please Anna and maybe – make her proud of her daughter. After much toing and froing, she was rather pleased with her final selection, a muted designer silk outfit of a soft mulberry colour – a strappy top with softly draped pants reminiscent of pyjamas. A matching cropped top of the softest silk in a slightly lighter colour completed the look. Well almost completed the outfit. All she needed to find were the killer heels she had planned to wear. Eventually found – under the bed where they may or may not have been hidden by a certain unhappy hound, who was now staring at her mournfully. He recognised going out clothes when he saw them.

Sabine popped her head into Stella's room where she was putting the finishing touches to her outfit.

'Not only do I look amazing but I'm ready early! Now isn't that a surprise?' said Sabine as she swirled around to display her gorgeousness. 'And look at you! Don't you look stunning. I would kill for those curls – no need for you to slave with a styling wand. It's so not fair. And that is the most amazing colour dress! You should forget all other colours and stick to red forever.'

Stella gently patted her hair which was a mass of soft curls and then smoothed down her dress. Sabine was correct. The deep red of her full skirted halter necked 50's style dress made her olive skin glow and her deep chocolate eyes shine.

'It's one I picked up in that vintage shop just around the corner. I've been dying to wear it for ages. It's not the sort of thing I could wear to court – imagine how I would be received if I turned up like this?'

'Hah! Might make the day less boring and guarantee a favourable hearing from the judge! Come on. Max will be here any minute. Where are your shoes? Are these the ones?'

Sabine held up a pair of red shoes with black spots.

Max was on time – of course. His reaction when Sabine opened the door was not what she expected. Not approval. Instead, disapproval was clearly visible on his features.

'Are you wearing that? Looks like pyjamas to me. Is that the best you can do? And what will your mother think?'

Sabine stepped back from the door - doubt flooding in. Was Max correct? Had she really got it so wrong?

'She will think her daughter is gorgeous – as always,' the cool tones of Stella's voice wafted down the corridor. Stella came into view and as she came close, she gave the dumbstruck Sabine a quick hug.

'I suppose it is a bit much to expect a barrister to be on top of fashion. After all, look at the silly outfits you barristers wear in court. What our young Sabine is modelling tonight is the latest in evening attire. SO on trend. She may indeed be the star of the show,' said Stella smiling reassuringly as her housemate.'

It didn't matter that Max, realising his error spoke rapidly to apologise and acknowledge his fashion ignorance. It was too late. His barbed words had struck, inflicted pain and lingered. Sabine's pleasure in her appearance was destroyed. No longer looking forward to showing off to her mother all she wanted to do was crawl into a corner and hide.

But that was not to be. The ride across to Vaucluse was silent. When they arrived Stella was first out of the car and led Sabine up the front path while Max having made sure the car was locked, followed silently some way behind.

'Don't let grumpy there spoil your night. This is your mum's special night. Let's focus on her – and the food – and the wine. Come on cheer up!'

Sabine forced a smile. It was hard to be sad when the evening was so warm and still – inviting happiness and dispelling her gloom. The twinkling lights lining the path sparkled a welcoming way forward towards the murmuring sound of a crowd having fun. They climbed the front steps and entered the front door into a wide tiled entry. Anna who had been speaking to a couple Sabine vaguely recognised as near neighbours, broke away and glided across the room towards them.

'Dearest Stella and my darling daughter. Don't you both look divine. Stella come give me a kiss. It's been too long. I hope my daughter hasn't been keeping you away?'

'Not at all and thank you for inviting me.'

Anna kissed Stella and Sabine in turn. Then gazing at her daughter, she spoke with tears glistening in her eyes:

'Forgive me but you look more and more like your father. Especially in that colour. That sort of mulberry colour was one he favoured. Something to do with making his eyes seem bluer – and it certainly does that for you. And evening pyjamas too? So stylish and absolutely on trend.' Turning her head and peering around she continued: 'And Max? Where is he? I hope you have brought him. I do so want to meet him.'

'And meet him you shall,' Max's deep voice was heard as he entered the room appearing from the outside shadows.

Max was aware he had to be on his best behaviour and not antagonise Sabine's mother. The evening had already got off to a bad start. Whilst he knew he was not completely forgiven he hoped with time he might be able to rectify things with Sabine. And it certainly would help if he was able to impress Anna.

At first sight he found it hard to believe Anna was Sabine's mother. The physical differences were so striking. Anna fine boned, petite and dark haired. Sabine so tall, athletic and fair. If it wasn't for the fact that he had met Judge Faulkner he would have been convinced Sabine was adopted.

And their manner was so different. Anna was charm personified. Softly spoken and keenly interested in Max. Speaking to her now he found himself opening up and divulging much more than he generally did when questioned. Even her words of sympathy about the loss of his mother were not resented, as they were delivered with such a genuine feeling of empathy and compassion. What an amazing mother she must have been and such a contrast to his own. It was clearly obvious that Anna loved her daughter. He watched the loving expression on her face as she gazed across the room at Sabine who was engaged in a vivacious conversation with a gentleman who looked vaguely familiar. A client or fellow lawyer perhaps? Or someone from the Party?

'I feel a bit anxious leaving my daughter. We've never been far apart and as her mother I can't help but worry, although I know she is an adult and has always been very independent.'

*Worry? A parent worry about an adult child?* This was a new concept to Max. But he saw an opportunity to impress and dived in.

'I understand perfectly and please don't be concerned. I will take good care of your daughter. Trust me – she is safe with me. I know it's a big change for both of you, but I will let you know if I feel in any way worried that she is not coping. It's a promise.' Max smiled in what he hoped was a reassuring manner.

'Max that is such a comfort,' Anna tapped him on the arm as she looked deeply into his eyes. 'Just knowing you are here keeping an eye on Sabine is such a relief to me. We mothers worry you know – even when our baby has all grown up. She will always be my baby.'

*Really?* Max was at a loss for words. This was making him feel nauseous, but before he could excuse himself Anna darted away with a murmured apology about the need to see to the caterers. Max glanced across the room at Sabine who remained in intense conversation with the same man as before. Should he go and rescue her – or should he talk to the gorgeous redhead who was heading his way with two glasses in her hands and a welcoming smile on her face. A face from his not too distant past and still a welcome face. Now why was she here tonight? Surely her circle of friends didn't include any of these pillars of establishment that were crowding the rooms. But then again – women of her expertise were known to pop up in the most unusual surroundings. A friend of the Judge's perhaps?

Across the room the conversation had moved from banal pleasantries to an intense interrogation.

'Your mother tells me you are seeing Max Sumner?'

At Sabine's nod he continued; 'A bright young man that and one that I predict will go places. I suppose it is no secret to you that he is seeking pre-selection for the seat of Sydney in the next State election?'

She nodded.

'Yes. Max has mentioned that to me. I don't know much about politics, but I would have thought he would be an asset to any government.'

Sabine felt an obligation to be supportive of Max's ambitions even though she had yet to think too deeply about it. Politics was such a mystery to her. In fact, Sabine was fairly sure she didn't care for it at all. Ask her to name the current and previous Prime Ministers and she would have struggled. Ask her who won last year's Eurovision competition and she would have answered correctly and without hesitation.

'An asset – most certainly. A lawyer with life skills will always have a place in the party. And with a partner such as you, hailing from a legal dynasty – well it doesn't get better than that. Been together long, have you?' the beady eyes peered intently at her – as if he was focussed on testing the truth of her response.

'Well, Max has been a part of the family for quite a while – he was an associate of my fathers,' a slightly misleading response but she was reluctant to indicate how short an acquaintance it had been. Her response appeared to be acceptable and all that was now required was to try and look interested in the deluge of spit delivered anecdotes about the speaker's own political career. As if she cared. However, Sabine supposed looking attentive would have to be good practice for contact with all the other people she would have to endure if Max did decide to launch into a political career. Opening nights and events with important people might be an inducement to a political life but it was likely the boring bits might outweigh them. Did she love Max enough to commit to this? Looking across the room at him deep in conversation with a rather glamorous woman who looked strangely familiar she was struck anew as to how handsome Max was. His head tilted attentively towards the woman as she gesticulated, then laughed. Max laughed in return smiling deep into her eyes. She supposed she would have to get used to other woman flirting with her man – but not tonight!

And especially not in her own home. With a muttered *excuse me* Sabine left the still talking gentleman and headed to Max's side.

'Hello there. I don't think we've met?' Sabine smiled at this woman, while placing her hand possessively on Max's arm.

'No. I don't think we have. I'm Phoebe.' The woman's smile revealed perfectly straight teeth but didn't extend to her beautifully made-up eyes. An elegant hand was presented for a limp handshake and then with a wave the woman glided off, clearly disinterested in continuing her conversation now that Sabine was present.

'Did I interrupt something?'

'No. not at all. I was just making polite conversation.' His eyes twinkled 'I saw you were cornered by one of the Liberal Party heavies. I was just about to rescue you, but it looked like you were holding your own.'

'Oh my god. He was awful. Do you really want to go into politics? He gave me the third degree. I didn't realise that I would also be put to the test if you want to be preselected.'

Max grimaced: 'Sorry about that. But they do trawl through my life – and as you are part of it, I suppose they will be wanting to know you better.'

*Part of his life?* Sabine leaned into him as emotion flooded through her – a feeling of delight as she anticipated a shared future mixed with some dread when she realised what that shared future might entail.

Then with the tapping of a spoon on a glass in the time-honoured manner of attracting attention it was time for speeches. To Sabine's delight she saw that Andre was the Master of Ceremonies. Until now Sabine hadn't been aware that he was present. She assumed that he must have been out of sight and part of the raucous crowd outside on the terrace. The speeches were short, witty and at times emotional. When it became Anna's turn to respond she spoke quietly and with feeling:

'Thank you everyone. Not only for being here tonight but also for welcoming me to this life when I married the Judge. It was hard to leave the ballet world behind, yet with your support – and of course the loving support from my late husband – I was able to create a new life. A life I wouldn't have missed for the world. And thank you to my daughter who has shared the journey with me.'

Anna beckoned her daughter inviting her to come and stand by her side which she did. Arm in arm with Sabine Anna continued: 'Now please forgive me if I sound a bit emotional, but even though I feel sad to leave this beautiful home I know I will carry with me your friendship and all the precious memories of special times over the years as I head into the next exciting stage of my life. And exciting it will be. I feel both excited and terrified to once more become involved in the ballet world. This is something I thought would never again be part of my life and I will do all I can to help Andre make the ballet company thrive.'

Raising her glass Anna continued: 'I would like to propose a toast – to Andre and the Classical Ballet School. Long may they continue.' Anna beamed her joy at the audience. And they responded with cheers and many a raucous toast in return.

It was very late by the time the party wrapped up. It was only when people were starting to drift off that Sabine finally abandoned her duties as hostess' daughter and wandered out onto the terrace. The emotion of the evening and the knowledge that soon her childhood home would no longer be part of her life was getting to her and she felt like she needed some time on her own. A quick glance reassured her that Max wouldn't miss her. He was engaged in what looked like it was a serious conversation with the same boring man who had cornered her earlier. Well, Max was welcome to him!

Perching on the stone wall that edged the terrace she gazed thoughtfully at the lights sparkling around the harbour and the distant view of the harbour bridge. A magical sight that she had always taken for granted. Now it was being taken away from her Sabine knew she would miss this view.

'Ah there you are,' Andre perched on the stone wall next to her. His outline indistinct in the semi-lit darkness of the terrace. But she knew in an instant who it was.

'I didn't expect to see you here tonight?'

'Wouldn't miss it for the world. Flew up from Melbourne especially.' Andre's voice softened as he took in the pensive expression of the young woman slumped on the stone wall.

'Big changes are afoot – both for your mum and you.'

Feeling choked up it was all Sabine could manage to deliver an affirmative grunt.

'In many ways I expect it will be harder for you than for your mother. The person left behind has the reminder of the loss – the hole left in their life by the loss of a loved one – and also the loss of your childhood home.' A sniff confirmed the accuracy of Andre's assessment. 'Your mother on the other hand will have many distractions in the coming days – moving, settling and the challenges of finding her place in the Company. But I'm sure she will still miss you – her only daughter. Don't forget the flight to Melbourne is no big deal and if you do decide to pop down – and I sincerely hope you will visit often – trust me, I will make sure there are lots of exciting things for you to see and do. Maybe- just maybe you might fall in love with the city as I have done and move there permanently. Lots of legal jobs down here that might tempt you.'

'Andre you are such a sweetie to care. Who knows? I might just take you up on that offer. And you might regret that.'

'Never!'

Arm in arm they wandered across the terrace and through the open French doors into the lounge room to discover a room almost empty of party goers. Various catering staff fussed around collecting empty glasses, plates and the serviettes discarded by the horde.

Anna was by the front door farewelling some neighbours who were at the tearfully emotional stage. With a quick hug Anna pushed them through the door while assuring them she would keep in touch and then returned to the lounge room.

'Keep in touch Ma? Really?' asked Sabine. 'They were right pains in the neck. Always complaining about something – even about my dog. Can you imagine anyone complaining about him?'

'Indeed,' said Anna giving her daughter a quizzical smile. 'But it is much easier to be kind to troublesome neighbours when I am about to leave them far behind. Who knows – in time I might even hold fond memories of them? Then again – perhaps not. Come on let's go into the family room and have one last drink. It would be nice to have a quiet time with just you – and Max and Stella of course.'

There was still one bottle of champagne left which they shared between them after Max proposed a toast thanking Anna for her hospitality – for the great company, delicious food and very impressive champagne.

'It was nothing,' Anna demurred. 'We've just drunk the last of the Judge's champagne and it couldn't have gone to a better cause. I think tonight went well – don't you?'

Everyone agreed. Sabine who had been puzzled by the number of guests she didn't recognise quizzed her mother.

'Quite a few were from various committees I have been involved in over the years – and their partners – many of those I don't know either. And there were the neighbours, my coffee and gym friends and a few of your father's colleagues whom I thought I should invite. Yes, and Andre – so lovely of him to make the trip and he is going to drive with me to Melbourne once we have finished packing up here. He said something about me not being safe to drive such a long distance on my own. As if I'm an old lady!' scoffed Anna.

'I heard that!' said Andre coming into the room from the kitchen where he had been gossiping with some of the staff. Judging by the merriment coming from that room it sounded like a mini party was in full flow.

'Don't mind them,' said Andre. 'They're just eating the leftovers.'

Andre dismissed Sabine's expressions of gratitude about helping her mother. 'It's nothing – a road trip with your mother will be lots of fun. I'm going to book a fancy place to stay at Beechworth on our first night so we can travel at leisure. Just like the old days hey Anna when we toured, but this time we will be travelling in style.'

Anna and Andre smiled at each other lost in a glow of shared memories. It was clear to Sabine she need not worry about her mother. Anna's happiness was assured, with Andre so devoted to her wellbeing.

'Are you OK?' asked Max as he drove Sabine and Stella home. He had already made it clear he would not be staying the night as he had a case starting on the Monday and would need to prepare all Sunday. This just added to Sabine's melancholy. Her mother abandoning her and now her man was too busy to spend the night with her. His patting her leg was no consolation and she turned and peered out the side window, staring at nothing in particular.

'Maybe if I get everything organised in the morning, I might be able to see you in the afternoon? I'll let you know.'

'It's fine. I've already promised Fran that I would babysit tomorrow so she can have a break. Don't worry.' Sabine didn't want to sound petty, but she couldn't help it. 'Maybe you can find some time in your busy schedule to see me later in the week.'

Telling Max not to bother escorting her inside she proffered her cheek for a kiss before sliding out of the car and with a token wave she left Stella to bid Max farewell.

'That was a bit harsh,' said Stella once they were inside and fending off an ecstatic Grover.

Sabine shrugged. 'And his not liking my outfit wasn't?'

Later as she lay in bed reviewing the evening's events Sabine did wonder if she had been the teeniest bit mean in her treatment of Max. After all it was the first time he had met her mother and he might have been a bit nervous. Perhaps she should ring Max to apologise or at the least thank him for his company and wish him a good night? Yes, that would be the proper thing to do. But when she did so, her call went through to Max's voicemail. Rather than leave a message she hung up and stared at her phone thoughtfully. Max always had his phone turned on. It was something he had very proudly told her in their early days together – she thought it was a sign of his sense of how important he was.

Much later in the evening as she dozed off, the image of that red haired woman came into Sabine's mind. What was her name? Phoebe – that was it. Now she remembered why she looked familiar. That was the same woman Max had acknowledged at the bar that night when they were at the new pub around the corner.

# Chapter Twenty One

# A visit and that bat phone

Fran lived with her husband and baby at Dover Heights in the Eastern Suburbs. Not that far as the crow flies from Sabine's home in Darlinghurst, but on a busy weekend afternoon it seemed a long way away. The traffic crawled along New South Head Road so as to delay an already late Sabine. Just as she was contemplating calling Fran to apologise for her lateness and indicate she was still on her way, the traffic cleared and she was on the move once again.

Even so she was a good half an hour late by the time she pulled up outside a white two storey house set on the high side of the street with views towards the harbour. Sabine rang the doorbell then stood back and looked for a sign of life. Nothing. She pressed the button again and for good measure also knocked on the multipaneled front door.

Then from behind her the sound of determined footsteps. Turning she found a swarthy man bearing down upon her carrying a rake, a frown and a glower that indicated perhaps she was not a welcome visitor.

'You. You are not welcome,' he spat out the words in strongly accented English. 'See the sign,' he said as he pointed at a notice on the brick wall by the front door – *Hawkers not welcome*. 'Go. We do not buy anything.'

He pointed towards the path: his intent clear and a threat obvious in his posture as he moved closer to Sabine.

'But ...'

'No buts. Go!' Again the pointing with his hand.

Sabine tried to swallow her terror. This strongly built little man might be scary, but she towered over him. Pulling herself up to her full height of six foot she spoke slowly and loudly as if speaking to someone who was hard of hearing. Maybe that would calm him down or if nothing else alert Fran to her presence.

'I'm Sabine. I work with Fran and she is expecting me. We were in contact this morning and she invited me over. I'm a little bit late and I'm hoping she hasn't given up on me.'

The man thumped the rake hard on the path. Not placated at all. But before he could say anything further the door slowly opened revealing Fran with baby strapped into a carrying pouch. She took in the situation at a glance, but with the calm of someone clearly familiar with such situations gave a quick shake of her head towards Sabine and then turned towards her husband.

'It's alright Arlo. This is Sabine. We work together. I mentioned she might pop in today – remember? We might go for a bit of a walk down to the reserve and with a bit of luck Mia here might nod off. We won't be long and that will give you time to finish your gardening.'

Without a word Arlo nodded, glared at Sabine then turned on his heels and headed around the side of the house.

'I'm awfully sorry about that,' said Fran. 'He doesn't like visitors – has always been a bit funny about strangers, but lately it is becoming worse. I think he doesn't like to share me nor Mia with anyone. It's possible you being so tall, frightened him a little. Normally he is much more aggressive.'

'More aggressive? Fran, he really frightened me. I thought he was going to take a swing at me with that rake. I was already to sprint down the path.'

'I had been watching out for you and planned to be at the door when you arrived – but then ...'

'Yeah, I know – but then I was late. Sorry about that. Punctuality is not something I'm known for.'

By now they had reached the corner and turned into another street which headed in the direction of the clifftop. Arriving at a nearby reserve they followed a path until they found a bench to sit on - strategically positioned with enjoyment of the watery view in mind. But neither woman was focussed on the view. Instead, they turned to each other. Clearly something had to be said. Sabine in typical manner dived in first.

'Fran I've been worried about you for a while but thought if I said something you would think me way out of line. But after what happened just now – well I think we really do need to talk.'

'Worried. About me?'

Fran's reaction was puzzling as if she thought she had kept everything hidden.

'Yes. I've seen the bruises on your neck you keep hidden with scarves and those polo neck jumpers you wear.'

Fran's hand crept tentatively up towards her neckline which not surprisingly was hidden today by the high collar of her knitted jumper.

'Bruises around the neck don't happen by accident and I can't help but notice that lately you seem really pale and subdued. And after seeing how your husband greeted me, I'm wondering if everything is alright with you. Are you OK? Do you want to tell me what's going on. More importantly what really worries me is whether you are feeling safe?'

Fran shook her head.

'Thanks Sabine. I appreciate your concern, but I can handle this. Arlo has always been a bit insecure and difficult but lately he has ramped up his aggression. Probably something to do with me having little Mia here. Life has changed. This little baby has now become my priority and not him. And maybe my success with my job might also be another factor that is stoking his fears. He has always been rather competitive. You see, his gardening business is not flourishing. His people skills – or lack of them tend to put people offside.'

She turned and smiled at Sabine who was staring intently at Fran - concern etched on her features.

'Please don't worry yourself. I've known Arlo for years and I can handle him. He will settle down once he is used to sharing me with his daughter. Little Mia needs to grow up knowing her father. I should know. Mine shot through when I was a toddler. I need to give this my best shot. I will take care and he is OK if I stay submissive and let him think he is boss. Speaking of being boss I should head back. He will be wondering what I have been telling you and it's important that we are seen to return as if we are chatty and smiley – like we have been on a social outing.'

'Alright but promise me you will call if at any time you need help?'

'Of course.' Fran smiled.

'It's helped just being able to be open about my situation with you. I know you can't change things but having you on my side makes me feel so much more confident. But please keep this to yourself. Things will improve with time. I'm sure of that.'

Fran looked down and peered at the squirming shape in the pouch.

'I think this little one is almost ready for her next feed. All the more reason to return before she starts crying. Trust me you don't want to hear that. Young Mia has excellent lungs.'

Arlo appeared as soon as they came close to the house. Presumably he had been looking out for their return. Fran taking care to keep the conversation light thanked Sabine for coming and said she hoped they would see each other soon.

Arlo, suspicion obvious on his face said 'Hang on a minute. I thought you were workmates?'

'We are,' smiled Fran reassuringly 'but Sabine is now working in a different area and days can go by before we catch sight of each other. I hope you will come and visit again now you know where to find us. Isn't that right Arlo?'

Now that Arlo was reassured that Sabine had a minor part to play in Fran's life, he became more civil. His farewell was delivered with a grudging invite to pop in again – but only after ringing first – new baby and all that. Dredging up a slight smile he waved goodbye then turned away leaving Fran to hug her friend and whisper her thanks.

As she drove away Sabine pondered the situation. She already knew from her own experience that relationships were tricky. But this one seemed trickier than most. She just hoped Fran was being accurate when she said she could handle Arlo. There seemed little Sabine could do for Fran – except be there for her if and when things turned bad. Somehow, she thought it was only a matter of time.

\*\*\*

Next morning Sabine found herself sharing a lift with Rhys. Before Rhys could launch into his praise of the perfect surf conditions he had enjoyed that morning she spoke:

'Rhys I know we've only got a minute before we reach our floor and I don't want to break any confidences, but I just wanted to say I'm really worried about Fran's wellbeing. I'm not sure things are going well at home and wanted to check if you are aware of this.'

Rhys nodded. 'I can see you feel uncomfortable. No need to say anything more. Fran has shared with me and I'm doing all I can to support her in whatever she chooses to do. She has my number on speed dial. I can't do anything further at this stage apart from making sure she has access to the best support and advice. You've done well to speak to me about this. Leave it with me and I won't let on we have spoken.'

At that, they reached their floor, and each headed in separate directions down the corridor. Rhys walked slowly as he pondered what to do next: He realised that things must be bad if even a junior lawyer, such as Sabine had noticed the state Fran was in. Of course, he cared for Fran's wellbeing, but he knew some in the firm would be more concerned about how this could affect the firm's reputation if news of Fran's experience with domestic violence became known. For domestic violence it certainly was. Rhys was certain that concern for their colleague's security would be considered less important by some of his colleagues than concern for the possible impact on the firm's finances and public image.

Sabine, on the other hand was feeling relieved now that her worries had been shared with Rhys, and he as the responsible adult would surely know what to do. She certainly didn't and anyway she needed all her reserves to focus on the week ahead. For this was the week she was rostered on to be in charge of the bat phone.

'It's no big deal,' reassured Penny as she handed over the mobile phone on Monday afternoon. 'Make sure you keep it charged and with you at all times. If you are asked any tricky questions, you know ones to which you don't know the answers, just ring me straight away and if you can't get hold of me call Mei. You have the phone until Friday afternoon then I will take it back for the weekend. With a bit of luck you won't get any calls. That often happens.'

Sabine tentatively received the phone, holding it as if it was some precious religious icon.

'It's just a phone Sabine. Not something that is about to electrocute you!'

Monday night was quiet – not one call came through on the dreaded *bat phone* although she received several calls on her own phone – two from Max organising time to meet and one from her mother in a fluster about what to store and what to give away.

'Ma, don't fuss. Whatever you decide is fine with me. I've taken what I need which in the end wasn't much. I promise I will wave you off on your big adventure on Thursday, so long as you don't get weepy on me. I don't think I could cope with that and I'm sure Andre won't want two emotional females on his hands.

Arrangements made and agreed Sabine then went to bed. Maybe all the carry on with the bat phone was just exaggeration. Or at least she hoped so. But then came Tuesday night. No sooner was she home from work and about to take the dog out for a walk when the dreaded *bat phone* rang. She let it ring three times before mustering up courage Sabine answered the phone with a tentative hello. Then continuing in a stronger tone of voice:

'*Smithtons*. Hello. Sabine speaking.'

'Sabine? It's Sam here. Sam Menzies.'

'Thank goodness it is you. I'm in charge of the phone this week and have been in an absolute panic about what to do if this phone rang. But I guess you aren't ringing for a chat. How can I help you? And please don't get cross if I don't know the right answer. This is my first time in charge of the *bat phone* after all. I'm a *bat phone* virgin you might say.'

At this Sam chuckled and then launched into describing his problem.

'I've just written an article which my editor has suggested I run past you to check it isn't defamatory. OK if I email it to you now?'

'Sure. I'll review it and get back to you as soon as I can. How long do I have?'

'Not long at all. A response straightaway would suit me.'

*I'm sure it would*, muttered Sabine to herself as she discontinued the call.

Sabine read the article focussing intently on each word. It was an article intended for the weekend paper and was mainly concerning on the epidemic of sexual abuse in the entertainment industry. By and large it was straightforward and outlined details of various interviews with a number of actors from screen and TV. She scanned the details of those interviews – which outlined general experiences of harassment during these individuals' careers but were a bit hazy about names, dates and the perpetrators. So far so good. Then she read several paragraphs towards the end of the article and she realised that this must have been the part that had prompted the editor to suggest Sam obtain a second opinion.

It was a report on a recent court case – a hearing currently underway which was subject to a suppression order preventing identification of the defendant in the media. The defendant who was apparently a pillar of society had applied for and been granted permission to keep details of his identity confidential. This was on the basis that there could be adverse consequences to his reputation if his identity was made known, yet he was subsequently found innocent. Trouble was that anyone reading Sam's analysis of the case and the circumstances of the harassment could identify the defendant. Sam had been a bit too particular in his description of the event where the harassment had been alleged to have taken place and whilst the identity of the defendant had not been divulged, the identity of the victim was.

Sam answered on the first ring.

'Sam it's a really interesting article and I can see you have put a lot of research into it. The stories of some of the people you have interviewed are amazing and their courage in coming forward is to be commended. I have no comments on that part of the article.'

'But?'

'But the part about the court case and the suppression order might need revision unless you want to be done for contempt of court. Even I can work out the identity of the individual. And if I can then it's a fair bet most of your readers will be able to as well. And then I will have to visit you in gaol. Mind you there might be some interesting stories to write about your time there.'

'So, what do you suggest I do?'

'Well to start with, what is the purpose of that part of your article, and does it need to remain?'

'Yes, it does. I wanted to show that it is possible to prosecute for such bad behaviour and that there are consequences. You know a sort of moral to the tale – that the times are a changing, and such perpetrators will be brought to justice.'

'But does that mean you have to use this case? Can't you find one where someone has already been convicted and there is no suppression order?'

'If you can find one, I'll use that instead. You have twenty minutes.'

Twenty minutes of furious research followed – and just as she was about to admit defeat, she found it. Not only was it a relevant decision but it was a recent one that involved a high-profile actor being convicted of abuse of another young actor. Perfect.

'Sam. I've got something and I'm emailing you the details now. It's a recent court decision and not subject to any suppression order. It will do as an example that harassers won't get away with it and not only that it will keep you out of gaol. No need to thank me now.'

The phone call over Sabine leant back and thoughtfully patted Grover, who had been anxiously sitting on her feet. He could sense the sudden relaxation in his mistress. Her tension easing and then with a grin she spoke:

'We did it Grover. My first phone consultation with a real-life client – I nailed it!'

# Chapter Twenty Two

# The Proposal

Max spoke on and on. Some part of her could appreciate his melodic voice and perfect enunciation. It was almost hypnotic – a thing of beauty – something to be appreciated without even having to pay attention to the content of what he was saying. No wonder Max had such success with jury trials. She bet those juries, especially the ones populated by women found themselves lulled into a state of almost hypnotic bliss – induced without conscious thought into agreeing with whatever Max suggested. Not listening and just lost in the beauty that was Max and his voice, she found herself smiling back at him as Max continued. It was the cramping of her cold and wet feet that finally brought Sabine to attention and made her pay proper attention to what Max was saying.

Max was proposing. Proposing marriage that is – not proposing chocolate cake for dessert. Mind you she thought the chocolate cake she could see being devoured by the people at the neighbouring table was well worth selecting. But marriage?

Max had paused in his dissertation. He looked at her expectantly. His dark eyes soft with emotion and his expression hopeful. Clearly a response was required. But what could she say? Maybe she did want to marry him? But then again it seemed all too soon. Couldn't they just continue as they were – although hopefully with warmer and drier feet. That would be so much better.

The silence was dragging out. She knew he expected her to say something in response– but what? And as always, in typical Sabine manner and without giving it any further consideration she dived right in.

'Max. You are such a dear. I feel totally overwhelmed. This is so unexpected.'

*Slow down Sabine. You are gushing.* She reached across the table and took his hand in hers. That touch as he clasped her still slightly chilled hand in his comforting grip felt welcome and warming. If only he would do the same for her freezing cold feet which were rapidly become painful with cramp. Trying not to squirm she continued.

'I honestly don't know what to say. You've taken me by surprise.'

'It's easy. Say yes,' urged Max, anxiety evident in his expression.

'Yes - maybe,' pondered Sabine. 'It's just I've never thought of marriage. I'm too young and I guess I always thought of marriage as for people much older than me.'

Max went to speak but before he did, she continued: 'Yes, I know mum was my age when she married but that was a different century and it all seems so final. Can't we just live together? You know I love you.'

*At least, I think I do she thought.*

'Can't we work up to it? Give me time Max. I'm sorry if this is not quite the answer you want, but I think I'm in shock from getting drenched. Chocolate cake might help you know,' she said smiling at the hovering waiter.

'Then chocolate cake it is.' Max beckoned the waiter over and placed their order. One serve of the chocolate fudge cake with two spoons. Sabine tried to keep smiling. She would have liked a serve of cake of her own. But never mind - at least Max was distracted now waving at a couple entering the restaurant who were heading their way.

Greetings exchanged it was clear this couple were of some importance to Max and from the conversation Sabine soon understood why. The man was somehow connected with Max's preselection which had been voted on that night and it was evident from the congratulatory tone that Max had got the gig. Happiness all around. Thanks, given and received, along with effusive congratulations. A niggling thought – was that why he needed a fiancé? Surely a dating partner would be sufficient? But this was politics – always many steps behind the rest of the population with its acceptance of societal changes. Anyway, the chocolate cake had finally arrived and with it joy of joys – two glasses of champagne. The couple moving onto their table left Sabine and Max to the delights of dessert.

Perhaps it was the welcome news of his preselection providing a distraction or the sugar hit from consumption of cake, but it was obvious to Sabine that Max was on a high – a sugar high or a high brought about by the news of his preselection success? She didn't care. It was distraction enough from any talk of marriage. The rest of the evening passed happily enough. They had lots to discuss – largely about Max, his week in court and the upcoming election. Max expected the announcement of his preselection would occur in the coming days and he warned Sabine there might be some publicity. And maybe a photo opportunity – for the two of them of course. Sabine smiled sweetly accepting this was probably the start of a changed world for her. The thought of being stalked by the paparazzi as she commuted to work, dodging the traffic and no doubt being caught in the act of committing numerous traffic offences made her smile.

'You're smiling. What's so funny?'

'The thought of me being a politician's partner. That's hilarious and so unlikely. I'm clumsy, too tall and tend to blurt out whatever I'm thinking. I could be a liability.'

'Mmmm. You could be right. Definitely a need for media training and maybe someone to sort out your wardrobe. Some of your clothes are a bit out there.'

Sabine could feel herself bristling. She had been joking. Did he have to take everything so seriously. Then again – maybe Max was right. As a potential politician's partner or serious lawyer - whichever person she chose to be perhaps she could do with a bit of repackaging.

\*\*\*

Or this was how she explained it to her mother later that evening after Max had deposited her at her home with muttered promises to return later that night after he finished something that had *just come up at Chambers*.

'Ma now that Max has been preselected for next year's election and things are going so well at work. I'm starting to realise I might need a bit of help. You know to present myself in the best possible way —with a bit of a wardrobe makeover and maybe some media training – and learning to present myself better to become – well – a bit more like you. I sometimes wish I could be as elegant as you and to glide – not galumph around like a herd of hippos.'

'Sabine dear,' her mother's warmth was apparent in her voice. 'You are perfect just the way you are. It won't work if you try to be anything other than your true self. Trying to be something or someone else will just make you unhappy. I glide, as you call it, because of all those years of ballet training. It's now ingrained, and I couldn't walk any other way – even if I tried. Your galumph as you call it is just a display of your high energy and zest for life. And I must say it makes me happy to see you bounce around – as I'm sure it does to others. You bring a lot of joy to the world.'

This was what she would miss once her mother left town. Someone who believed in her no matter what. As if sensing what her daughter was thinking Anna continued:

'I'll only ever be a phone call away – or you can use that FaceTime that you like to use. Or perish the thought, you could come and visit me – and bring that dratted dog. They do let them catch the plane you know. Now my dear, Andre and I are leaving first thing tomorrow. I'm thinking we might swing past your place on our way out of town to say goodbye. But will you be up?'

'Grover and I wouldn't miss it for the world. What time?'

# Chapter Twenty Three

# Grover

True to her word Anna was early. Too early in the morning to beep the horn and wake the neighbours from their rest. So early a car park was readily found not far from Sabine and Stella's home. The metallic sound as she opened the front gate alerted Sabine to the arrival of her mother. She and Grover had snuck out of bed sometime earlier, leaving Max in a deep slumber. At the sound of that distinctive metallic screech, she bounded down the corridor and opened the door with a flourish then launched herself into Anna's arms while Grover frolicked around their legs almost tripping them up.

'Calm down – both of you. Sabine do control your dog. We don't want him waking up the neighbourhood.'

Too late as Grover bounded out the front door barking with excitement. A chase ensued and once her dog was corralled in her arms Sabine asked:

'Where's Andre?'

'In the car. This is just a drive past – remember. Not to say goodbye but just time for a quick kiss and cuddle. Now do not cry my dear. Think of it as I'm only going a short way down the road. Come say hello to Andre – and don't sniff.'

Sabine burying her tear-stained face in Grover's side followed as her mother chattered on about their plans for the day. Maybe a stop for coffee in Berrima, lunch at a gourmet pub further on and then the night at Beechworth to look forward to. Clearly no feelings of sorrow about leaving her home or daughter behind.

Andre seeing them approach jumped out of the car and greeted Sabine with a kiss on each cheek and a firm hug as if he was trying to convey his feelings of support for the soon to be abandoned daughter.

Anna finally sensing her daughter's distress promised to ring that evening once they were settled into their accommodation and also to keep in regular contact over the following days.

'I'll keep in touch – promise. I will make sure I share everything with you.' She smiled: 'I can't help feeling like our roles have reversed – I'm the irresponsible daughter running away and promising to keep in contact with her mother. And you, for once are the responsible one. Who would have thought it?'

They both laughed and with that laughter the mood lifted and it was then that a smiling Sabine waved at the pair as they drove away. She placed Grover gently on the footpath and they both returned to the house.

'You know Grover. Perhaps all this is for the best. I will miss mum of course. But it's not like we lived in each other's pockets. I can still go and stay and who knows? Maybe I might just like Melbourne. And if I say so in all modesty, it's all thanks to me that my dear mum has a chance of a new exciting life. How clever was I in locating Andre? Well I guess seeing as they didn't linger we could go for a walk before I wake that lazy Max.'

So much of what his mistress said was a sort of white noise. But out of that noise he heard one of the few words he recognised and a word that related to him. *Walk!* With a delighted woof Grover scampered inside to search for and locate his lead which he knew had to be part of the experience.

A short walk around the local park preceded by a stop at the local bakery, in accordance with their usual routine. Finger buns distributed as always to the homeless people in the park, but this time keeping back one to share with Grover and one for Max.

Max was still asleep when she returned home but a small dog who leapt onto the bed took care of that.

'Ouch you mongrel. Leave me alone.'

Max was not happy.

'Hey sleepyhead! Leave my dog alone. He's just pleased to see you. I've made you coffee and have a finger bun here for you. You've missed all the action. While you were snoring away mum and Andre stopped by to say goodbye.'

Sabine felt relieved that she could use that word without tearing up now that she had realised that it was not a final goodbye. She would see her mother again and hopefully in a much more exciting environment.

'And we've been for a walk and bought finger buns. See?' She said waving the finger bun in front of a recoiling Max. 'Exhibit A!'

'Eeew. Sugar for breakfast? Thanks, but no thanks. I'll stick with coffee.'

Sabine shrugged, trying not to feel miffed at such ingratitude.

'No worries. All the more for Grover and me. You may rest in bed – clearly you don't have to rush this morning, but I do – a busy day at work today. I'll just have a quick shower and get out of here. If Stella has left before you do, would you please make sure the front door is locked and the back door is ajar for Grover? Will I see you tonight?'

'Maybe' came the grunt from under the doona. She knew Max was not a morning person but she sensed his response might relate to other things. Maybe a sign he was grumpy about more than the disturbance to his rest by a small dog? Giving a mental shrug she decided to ignore it and focus on getting to work in time.

Which she did and to her joy of joys shared the lift with Fran.

'So good to see you, Fran. To be honest I really miss working with you and Rhys. Penny and Mei are fine, but they are just not you. The work is amazing yet somehow I think I need to work in a place where I really feel like part of a team and not a nuisance.'

Sabine panicked. Once again, she had blurted out too much information.

'Oh dear. I shouldn't have said that! Please don't tell them – and please keep it to yourself I beg you. It's just I feel like I can trust you and say what I really think. Where I am now is not all fun, despite what the promotional blurbs promised when I applied for graduate intake. I know it is frivolous of me but being part of a friendly team is just as important to me as doing interesting work. I suspect William might not understand that. I get the impression he thinks he is doing me a great favour by giving me the chance to work with his team.'

'It's OK Sabine. Really,' Fran patted her on the arm as if to convey reassurance. 'I totally understand how you are feeling. You can trust me not to blab. Anyway, the trust is mutual. I am really thankful that you have been there for me. Have you got a moment? I have a little something to share with you. In my office though – where we can't be disturbed.'

As Sabine followed Fran out of the lift and down the corridor she noticed something about Fran. Her outfit was different. A floral swirly dress with a toning cardigan draped around her shoulders. And for the first time in ages – no high neck and no scarf! Not only that but Fran also looked happy with a discernible bounce in her step.

As soon as they reached Fran's office and as she closed the door Sabine pounced:

'OK, what gives? You look happy.'

'I am.' Fran smiled – not a beaming, over the top smile - but a gentle, contented smile.

'You know it is thanks to you that things between Arlo and I have been sorted – hopefully sorted long term but who knows - maybe not. Still, at least I now know it is within both our powers to make positive changes.'

Seeing Sabine's puzzled look Fran elaborated. She explained how after Sabine's visit the other week, she realised her home life could not continue the way it was.

'I realised if things didn't change something terrible would happen. Both Arlo and I were in a bad way. I was barely holding it together and it would only take something minor to push me over and send me into a downward spiral – a breakdown or worse. And Arlo in his own way was barely coping. He was miserable and it was clear he didn't have the tools to deal with it. All he could do was rage as a way of showing his frustration. We've known each other since we were children, so I know him inside out yet for some reason I was powerless to help him. Being so exhausted and miserable myself I didn't have the energy to reach out to him. Our misery was feeding off each other - each day it was getting worse and worse. Your visit made me realise we had to do something. We had Mia to think about. She deserves to have two parents that are stable and focussed on creating the best family they can.'

'After you left Arlo's father arrived and found Arlo doing his usual rant, while Mia and I were hiding in the bathroom with the door locked. That was the circuit breaker. The intervention of his father made Arlo acknowledge his behaviour was unacceptable and that he and I both needed to seek help'.

'I had this week off on sick leave. Things have changed. Not quite overnight but the progress has been amazing. To start with Arlo's parents have moved in for as long as they are needed. They've been amazing helping with Mia so I can rest. It's so hard to think straight on two hours sleep a night. Now though, after getting some decent sleep that fuzzy feeling in my head has gone and I can start to think properly about our future and what needs to be done to give us both a proper support network. Not only that but Arlo has taken steps to learn how to behave better. He's joined a men's group and is getting counselling. So far, so good. We're talking more about our feelings and starting to work on how to operate as a team and not as individuals in conflict. It's funny but both of us felt we had to be responsible and not show any weakness, yet the ways we managed our distress and exhaustion were not healthy. I bottled it up. Arlo raged. Now that we've both acknowledged the challenges and are sharing our feelings, I'm hoping life will improve and Mia will have the best parents possible.'

Fran paused and looked out the window at the harbour scene displayed below. Somehow Sabine suspected she was not really seeing the amazing view but was instead focussed on her feelings.

'I know marriage has its ups and downs. My mother certainly said that about her second marriage and somehow, she and my stepfather are still together. I'm starting to think we might be heading for an up- and I'm feeling cautiously optimistic. Maybe in a few weeks I will feel more so.'

Fran staggered as she was enveloped in one of Sabine's enthusiastic hugs. But she didn't resist and instead surrendered to the emotion contained in her new friend's embrace.

'I'm so glad. You see Fran I was awfully worried about you but didn't know what to do.'

'It was enough just you being there and my knowing there was someone else not too far away who was concerned about Mia and me. You have no idea how much that has meant to me.'

'Well don't forget I'm still here for you and my offer is open. I will take care of Mia any time. Maybe that might be an occasion for you and Arlo to have a date?'

'You're on. And Arlo wants to see you. He says he owes you an apology for his behaviour. Maybe we could plan something in the coming weeks?'

'Sure. And how does Arlo feel about little dogs?'

'Don't push it Sabine. Introducing his daughter to a dog at this stage might be a step too far for Arlo!

\*\*\*

She may have been early arriving at work but after her heart to heart with Fran, Sabine was well and truly late for the team meeting that had been scheduled to start at 9am. Apprehensively she pushed open the meeting room door to find the eyes of all attendees swivelling around to stare as she entered the room.

'So glad you could join us at last Ms Faulkner,' said William in glacial tones, each syllable uttered with cut glass precision. He waved away her disjointed apologies as if they were of no interest to him and continued: 'No doubt one of my more punctual team members will bring you up to date regarding what we have been discussing but I have a client to attend to and I for one do not intend to keep them waiting. Punctuality has always been important to me. You might like to bear that in mind Ms Faulkner – that is if you intend on finding a permanent place in the Media Team.'

And with that the meeting was over and William still glaring at Sabine strode out of the room.

'Wow, that was a bit harsh,' sympathised Amy as they headed back to their desks. Sabine shrugged. After her discussion with Fran about what were real life issues a little temper tantrum by an old man who didn't even think to ask why she was late was totally irrelevant. No empathy there. His threat had no impact. As if she would want to work for such a person. Interesting work or not, a permanent placement in the Media Team no longer had any appeal.

As she sat down one of the Penny's assistants rushed over waving a note in her hand.

'I took a call on your phone while you were away from your desk. They said it was urgent.'

Sabine took the note and saw a number and a written scrawl – *ask for Claire, Inner City Vet Clinic - Urgent*. This didn't mean anything to her. Certainly Grover was overdue for his annual vaccinations. But unless there was a canine pandemic that shouldn't be classed as urgent.

Her call was answered with an officious person asking her to hold on – which she did, growing increasingly anxious with each minute's delay. When her call was finally answered Sabine identified herself and said she had been asked to call and speak to Claire.

'Ah yes. Grover's mum. Hold on a minute I'll put you through to the vet.'

*The vet? This must be serious.* And it was.

'Hello there. Is that Sabine Faulkner?'

'Yes, it is. But I don't know what this is about.'

'Of course. I suppose I should explain first that we have your dog. A local, possibly your neighbour brought him in about an hour ago. Luckily you have had him micro-chipped, so we were able to obtain your phone number and ring you.'

'And?'

'Oh of course. You don't know why he is here. Young Grover appears to have been hit by a car. The person that brought him in found him in the gutter – still conscious and obviously in pain. We've done a quick X-ray, and it would appear he has a broken leg and severe scraping along one side of his body – possibly where he was dragged along the road. I've given Grover some short-term pain relief to ease his distress, but I really want to know what you want me to do?'

'Do? Fix him of course. Whatever it takes. Do you need me to sign anything? Can I see him?'

'We will call you when it's time to come in and take young Grover home. I'll transfer you back to the front desk and they can sort out the paperwork. Then as soon as that is done Grover can go into surgery. Try not to worry. Grover is being kept comfortable and one of the nurses is keeping a close eye on him. We will let you know once he is out of surgery. He will be fine.'

She felt numb. Shock setting in she supposed. Yet it was important that she focussed on sorting out the permission forms that needed to be printed out, signed and sent back to the vet surgery. Grover depended on her to sort that out so he would be healed.

Yes, Grover depended on her. Why then was he out on the street and at risk of injury? How had he got out? A call to Stella did not help.

'He certainly was inside when I left. In the kitchen trying to scrounge scraps from Max who was at the table having breakfast. Maybe Max left the front door open by mistake? Although now I think of it – even if the front door was open the gate would be shut. It always swings shut anyway. I don't know.' Stella paused as if she was contemplating what could have led to Grover escaping into danger. Then as if sensing the troubled state of her housemate's mind she continued trying to calm Sabine.

'Anyway, the important thing is he was found and taken to the vets. It just goes to show what good neighbours we have in our street. Hopefully we can find out who was Grover's saviour and thank them. Sorry I have to go. I have another client to see. Ring me with updates though – or text. Bye.'

What to do? Sabine knew it would be impossible for her to do any work that day – her brain was focussed on one thing only – the wellbeing of her little dog. She no longer cared about the silly witness statement she had been working on, which yesterday afternoon had been her total focus. A quick chat with Penny when she explained what had happened and how she needed to leave work straight away. To her surprise Penny was understanding and gave her full approval:

'Of course, you have to go. Amy can take over that draft statement you were working on.'

Maybe this was Amy's chance to shine. After all, Amy still wanted permanent placement with this team even if Sabine did not.

No time to cycle home. Her bike could remain at work, securely locked in the basement bike rack. Once she was settled in a cab Sabine rang Max. Not surprisingly, it went through to his voicemail. No doubt he was in court – not for a hearing she thought. If it had been that he would have been leaving much earlier that morning for work. A directions' hearing maybe or a client conference? Whatever it was it didn't really matter. She left a message asking Max to ring when he got a moment and then focussed on what to do when she got home.

As she expected the front gate was firmly shut and immediately closed behind her once she walked through. The six-panel wooden front door likewise was shut and locked. Sabine stood before the front door and looked around. Gate shut, front fence secure and the two side fences that separated her front garden from the adjoining neighbours' gardens likewise solid and dog proof. How Grover escaped was a mystery. Sabine frowned. Maybe he had escaped out the backyard onto the laneway that ran behind the terrace houses. Once this laneway had served as access for the nightsoil carters in a previous century. With the installation of sewerage systems across the city these laneways now served as vehicle access to properties, an asset for an inner-city property and also as a meeting ground for the local cats. Given Grover's obsession with cats it was possible he may have escaped that way. She needed to check the backyard for possible means of escape. Which she then did. But there were none.

Sabine recalled the vet telling her she thought a neighbour had brought Grover in. Perhaps she should track down that neighbour. Her immediate neighbours whilst expressing concern over the *poor little doggy* said they knew nothing about it. But the neighbour across the road, Mabel, a long-time resident was able to tell her all.

'I didn't take your dog to the vets. That was the lad who lives four doors down. In that group house. But I saw what happened. Your little dog followed a man out of your house. And rather than put him back inside the man yelled at him, shooed him away and then he himself ran away - I assume so that little doggy of yours couldn't follow him. It seemed a bit odd to me as I know what good care you take of your little doggy and I was going to go outside and bring him into my house so he could spend the day with me. But I wasn't quick enough. Quick as a flash he took off chasing something – possibly a cat? And before I could get out the door I heard a screech of brakes, a thud and a yelp. The car, of course sped off. So awful. I saw the poor dear trying to crawl off the road and called out to the lad who was just leaving the house. He said he would take your little dog to the vets and I suppose he has. How is he?'

'I'm told he has a broken leg and is in surgery now. I should know more shortly.'

'Then a lucky escape my dear. Although probably best to take care it doesn't happen again. I think you should speak to the man of yours.'

'Believe me. I will.'

\*\*\*

'Hi Sabine. It's me. Sorry I missed your call. I was in court but I'm back now. Did you ring about tonight? Have you got anything planned or should we try and get a table at our favourite bistro?'

Sabine could feel her temper rising. He was acting just like it was any other day when the first topic of conversation concerned what to do for dinner. Reminding herself to stay calm she responded:

'I don't think I will be going out tonight. I will have a patient to attend to.'

'A patient? Stella? Is she OK?'

'No. I mean Grover. I will be busy with him.'

'Grover. What's happened to that mutt now?'

'It appears he has been run over. Somehow, he got out and was hit by a car.'

Like the best prosecutor Sabine fed out the information bit by bit with the intention of entrapping her victim.

'Got out? I told you he was trouble. Hit by a car, was he? Is he still alive then?'

'Yes. I couldn't see how he could have got out as the property is secure. Do you have any ideas?'

'No. Maybe the dog walker?'

Time to spring her ambush:

'I think not. You see it happened early this morning. After Stella left for work and probably just after the time you left. I made inquiries of the neighbours...' Sabine paused and let the silence deepen. Just to see what response would be drawn from Max.

'The neighbours? I thought they all worked?' His voice was becoming hesitant as if Max was starting to realise he was trapped.

'Not all of them. You see Mabel who lives across the road had a good view of you leaving the house being followed by Grover. She said she was puzzled when she saw you turn and shoo Grover away. As am I. What were you doing? I get that my dog might have escaped the house, but couldn't you have returned him? You have a key and you know where the spare key is hidden. Why Max – why?' Sabine could hear her voice close to breaking. Tears being held back as she tried to conquer her feelings of distress at the thought of her little dog suffering so.

Drawing on his philosophy that attack is always the best defence Max the barrister launched into his response. Not an explanation but a full-on assault.

'Yes, he got out and started to follow me. And no. I didn't let him back in. I was running late for court. Anyone can see that he's just a mongrel. A rescue dog and stray who rightly belongs on the street. He had no right to follow me and no right to be in your home. When I see how you pander to him it makes me sick. He gets far more attention than any human – eating your food and sleeping on your bed. It's disgusting. I had always planned that when we got married he would have to go. There is no room for him in our life. Not the life I plan. You will see. Eventually you will come around to my point of view. It's for the best if he goes. If you do still feel that you need a pet then I suppose I would be amenable to us acquiring a pedigree cat – something stylish with short hair that isn't too demanding and certainly does not sleep on our bed. Maybe a Siamese cat? I like their style. Not scruffy like your dog but elegant. Yes, that would be perfect.'

The only response was the sound of the call disconnecting.

'What else could I do?' Sabine said to Stella later that evening as they sat by the heater. Sabine seated on the floor next to a small dog lying on a sleeping mat, his back leg strapped in plaster and one side of his body scraped clean of hair and coloured orange from disinfectant wash.

'If I'd said anything I would have lost it and called him every name under the sun. I always suspected Max wasn't too keen on Grover, but I never realised he was actively planning on getting rid of him. Anyway, I'm off work for the rest of the week until I'm sure Grover can manage on his own and maybe I'll get the pet sitter to keep an eye on him next week – or maybe Mabel? Now that's a thought.'

Sabine patted her little dog who was still sedated but not that deeply sedated. One eye opened and he acknowledged his mistress with a gently thumping tail.

'I think it's time to change the locks,' said Sabine.

'It's that bad with Max then?'

'Possibly…most likely. I spoke to mum tonight. She says give it time to see how I feel once Grover has recovered. She seemed to think I should not do anything too hasty. As if!'

Stella smiled at her dear friend.

'Since when have you been anything other than hasty? My dear impulsive friend.'

# Chapter Twenty Four

# Unravelling

It was late. Too late to still be in the office. But there were documents to be redrafted and witness statements to be finalised before the witnesses came in first thing in the morning to sign them.

Sabine rubbed her eyes. She was so tired and hungry. Her stomach rumbled reminding her that dinner was long overdue. As it probably was for her little dog who was waiting for her to come home. It was time to leave. One more revision then she would call it a day, hail a cab and head home to her little friend.

Her mobile phone rang. For a heartbeat she wondered if it could be Max. No, that was all over – at least for now - and she must accept that. A glance at the phone display revealed an unknown number and hesitantly she accepted the call. It could be a client she supposed.

'Hello. Sabine Faulkner speaking.'

'Sabine this is Leanne Sumner Max's sister. Sorry to ring you so late but ever since I saw your photo in the social pages, I thought I should ring you. There are a few things that are bugging me and I think I need to share them with you.'

'Hi Leanne. I'm sorry we haven't met before. Somehow I had the impression that Max was estranged from his family.'

A snort on the other end of the phone.

'Estranged. Only because he chooses to be. You see we were never good enough for my precious brother. You see Mum and I so didn't fit into his grand plans. Once I read about you, I could see why he was so keen on you. You are the perfect partner for the Max he is planning on becoming. And I'm not sure if you know truly what you are getting involved in.'

'Oh, I'm now starting to find out' Sabine said with irony. But her comment was unheard by Leanne who rushed on:

'And then I see Max intends to stand in the upcoming election. He can't. A man like him shouldn't be inflicted on the electorate. He is only out for himself and will not represent or care for others. Believe me I know.'

Sabine was intrigued. Even though in her mind she and Max were no longer an item she knew he was desperately trying to win her back and sometimes she was tempted. His charm, charisma and physical abilities made him such a tempting package. If only he was less self-centred and more caring – of her and of her dog.

'Tell me more.'

And she did. The Max Leanne revealed – the real Max was quite a story. From his early rough days in the burbs when he learnt to defend himself from the bullies to how he changed his name and reinvented himself as a posh person at university. The name change came as a surprise to Sabine. Why would you bother doing that she wondered? His birth name David James Sumner seemed perfectly acceptable.

'I didn't realise it at the time but while he was at uni Max renewed contact with our father. I don't know how, but he then developed a nice little sideline supplying drugs sourced from our father to his fellow students. I suppose that explains why he had money and also why he became so popular. Charm and drugs – he had them in spades.'

'Drugs? But he doesn't do that now. Does he?'

'I'm not so sure. Ask his so-called call-girl friend Phoebe. I sometimes wonder if she is still a friend or if it is more. Maybe you don't care? But I'm fairly sure he is still using her to pass on the drugs. I have some photos I can share with you of him handing something to her. I did a bit of sleuthing last month – stalking you might call it and took the photos then.'

'Think about it. It makes sense if he is still doing a bit of something on the side. I know he is a reasonable barrister, but how else can you explain his multi-million-dollar apartment and fancy lifestyle, unless there is some other source of income? He wasn't born with money and has no trust fund.'

'Why are you telling me this?'

'Because you seem like a nice person and I don't want you to get hurt by being caught up in his schemes. I also think I have to act before he gets elected to Parliament. If he is successful at the election then there will be no stopping him and not only you, but also the community will suffer. I'm sending you some photos as soon as I hang up and if you want me to talk to anyone else – I don't know maybe a reporter or even the police – please pass on my number. I have to go now. Goodbye. I hope one day we will get to meet,' and with that Leanne hung up leaving Sabine slowly putting the phone down and staring into space as she wondered what she should do.

Should she contact the police? She wondered if doing so would change anything or would such information not be properly investigated but be dismissed as malicious tattle tales.

Sam? Maybe he was the person to contact? Perhaps this was a story for him? She knew from her experience at work that Sam would be scrupulously correct and would only publish a story that was factually accurate. With a ping she saw something had come in from Leanne. There were three photos – clear images of Max and the woman she recognised as Phoebe. Phoebe dressed in a skin-tight mini dress and towering stilettos and Max in his barrister robes. In one Max was clearly seen handing over a plastic bag containing something white. In the next Phoebe was passing over a bundle of cash. In the third photo Max was hiding the money in his robes while speaking heatedly with Phoebe. Serena knew that expression well. Max was not happy about something.

'Sam, it's Sabine Faulkner. I think I have a story you might wish to investigate. I'm sending you three photos now and a phone number for a Leanne Sumner. She has some information she might wish to share with you. I've just been speaking to Leanne and I've made a few notes. I'll send them to you as soon as I get home. It's important Sam. Bye.'

Job done. Her future sorted. Max would now be taken care of. Although she probably should do something official to make it clear to the public that they were no longer an item. In some respects, this was a pity, but she did need to take care and look out for herself. With a sigh Sabine turned off her computer, reached for her phone and headed for the lift. But not before turning out the lights. She was careful like that.

# Chapter Twenty Five

# Resolution

Like two players frozen in time in some contemporary portrait the two women stood still silently contemplating each other. Seconds passed with no sign of movement from either woman. Blue eyes met brown and stared – and stared. Until the brown eyed woman weakened and spoke first.

'Say that again?'

In response the other woman held out her mobile for the other to inspect. Silently she read whatever was displayed on the screen, her lips moving silently as she read as if to reinforce the meaning of the words. Her reading complete she looked up in horror as she passed the phone back to her companion.

'Beanie. You can't do that! No way! You can't send those notes to Sam! You'll destroy Max.'

As if in defiance to a challenge the other woman straightened, raised her chin and with a spoken 'Can't I?' pressed a button on the phone and whatever was in the message was sent. A triumphant grin as she pocketed her phone and then she held out her hand to the other.

Hand taken the dark eyed woman sighed.

'Oh, Beanie what have you done…'

# Chapter Twenty Six

# Afterwards

*(An Exclusive report from Sam Menzies our Sydney political correspondent)*
**Breaking News** – <u>**Lying to the Max**</u> – *Revealed. The deceitful life of Max Sumner Political Aspirant. Is he worthy of your vote?*

Who is Max Sumner the Liberal Party candidate for Sydney in the upcoming State election? Google him and you will find an impressive record. Education at a selective high school, an outstanding academic record at Sydney University and a successful career at the Sydney Bar. Recently engaged to the daughter of an eminent judge – Judge Faulkner – once his employer and now sadly deceased. His fiancée herself carving out an impressive career in the legal profession.

With that pedigree Max Sumner is one clearly destined for greatness in his new career – that of politics.

But is this the real Max Sumner? Dig a little deeper and questions start to arise….

*(From our legal correspondent)*
<u>**Big changes at leading legal practice**</u>

Changes are afoot at the law firm *Smithtons* following the shock resignation of partner Rhys Purcell who has left the firm to chase the waves up north at Byron Bay. There had been rumours for some time that Rhys had been less than satisfied with the culture in the firm. It's not surprising that the two female legal powerbrokers Fran Walshe and Sabine Faulkner have now stepped up to fill the vacuum created by Rhys' departure. Fran who has replaced Rhys as litigation partner has an extensive stable of A list clients and Sabine, who has recently been promoted to Associate is legal royalty. The daughter of Justice Faulkner who is now sadly deceased she brings to the position her extensive network of contacts in the legal and commercial world. Any perceived taint from her short engagement to that rogue Max Sumner seems to have washed away. The sky is the limit for this ambitious young lawyer.

*** 

Another long day at work for Sabine. And a busy one as always – a legal advice to finalise, team meetings, staff to supervise and now the added responsibility of keeping an eye on achieving her budget. She was beginning to realise that being elevated to Senior Associate level came at a cost – but so far it was a cost she was prepared to pay.

She answered her phone after the first ring. At this hour it had to be personal – or so she hoped.

'Hello Sabine speaking.'

'Hi there. It's Sam. Remember me?'

'Of course. My first *bat phone* caller. How could I forget the trauma of that call?'

'I was wondering – hoping even if you have time to catch up? I get it that you are now an important hot shot lawyer, but maybe you might like to meet for a drink or something? Just a thought.'

Sam – so straightforward and cheery – albeit in a slightly scruffy way. She wondered if he would still have that almost mullet hairstyle. Although style might be too generous a description. A happy soul. Nothing unknown about this man – this time there would be no hidden agendas. If nothing else she could do with a friend. Why not?

'Sure. How about tomorrow? I usually take the dog for a walk around Centennial Park and then we have brunch at the café there. Grover loves his Saturday croissant. Are you free tomorrow morning?'

'Absolutely! Tell me what time suits you and I will be waiting by your front gate. Just like any other stalker!'

As Sabine carefully hung up the phone she permitted herself a slight smile. Maybe life was looking up after all.........

www.ingramcontent.com/pod-product-compliance
Lightning Source LLC
Chambersburg PA
CBHW031230260626
47169CB00007B/2234